MS# 1600-4/3/2015
62,192 words

The Lollipop Murder

A novel by

Harley L. Sachs

ISBN   978-1939381-095

Books by Harley L. Sachs:

Novels

Queer Company
Never Trust a Talking Horse
The Gold Chromosome
Murder by Mail (Scratch—out!)!
Ben Zakkai's Coffin
The Search for Jesse Bram
The Mystery Club Solves a Murder
The Mystery Club and the Dead Doctor
The Mystery Club and the Hidden Witness
The Mystery Club and the Serial Widow
Conspiracy!
Murder in the Keweenaw
The Lollipop Murder
Betrayal
Retribution
Burnt Out
White Slave
Sam in Love
StopRape.com
The Accidental Courier

Collections of short fiction

Ahoy! Quarterdeck! (Irma Quarterdeck Reports)
Anna-Lena's Troll and other stories
Threads of the Covenant: The Jews of Red Jacket
Misplaced Persons

Non-Fiction

Freelance Non-Fiction Articles
The Misadventures of Cpl. Sachs
The 1957 Sachs Arctic Expedition
From Tent to Castle: Memoir of a Year-Long Honeymoon
IS
Chilly-Chilly BANG! How We Freelanced Through Europe's Coldest
*   Winter in a VW with a Kid*
Essays and Columns: 1992-2011
The Writing Life

Cartoons

Hunting the Mail Buoy and other hazards to navigation

Dedication

For the wannabes, a word of warning.

Acknowledgements

Thanks to Ulla and Belinda for their excellent suggestions and advice, to Prosecutor James Jenkins and police chief James Destramoe for legal tips.

One

An Invitation

"You've got a letter from your publisher," Devra said the moment Luther S— walked in through the door of their studio apartment in Portland, Oregon. What with Devra's student loan still not paid off, even with both of them working, a studio was all they could afford. It was similar to living in a motel room, not much unlike the temporary quarters otherwise homeless families were shunted into to keep them off the streets. The best Luther could do in the way of an academic job at Portland State University was an adjunct position, professorspeak for part time work, no benefits, large classes, no tenure and little hope.

At least an adjunct position left Luther time to polish that academic novel he'd used as a thesis at the University of Iowa writing program. Thanks to his University of Iowa roommate Charlie Broadbottom he had actually found a publisher. Charlie was a British transplant who used his accent to charm the University of Iowa coeds. He could be induced to imitate the BBC, an accent no known Brit outside of broadcasting ever affected. Besides being effective with girls, it helped him land a job with *Publishers' Journal*.

Broadbottom had steered Luther to an obscure publisher, Ira Ripov, who had actually taken him on for his stable of authors. Stroke of luck, sort of. It helped to have connections.

The result was Luther had a so-called debut novel, *Tracking Tenure*. Besides nearly crying with joy when he got his six author's copies, the book gave him a bit of hope. Bppks made money, right? He and Devra needed some extra income. At first the book had attracted a couple of reviews in publications but, though favorable, no fat royalties were forthcoming.

Being a so-called local author was enough to get him an appearance in the bowels of Annie Bloom's bookstore in Multnomah Village, but not at Powell's which would have been a real plum. Powell's was the largest independent bookstore on the West Coast if not the entire United States, and had a steady stream of top authors doing readings and signings for as many as a hundred devoted onlookers. Luther S-- was not in that class.

Ira Ripov had not paid an advance, Luther being a neophyte author, nor did he finance a book tour. The best Luther could arrange, besides the appearance at Annie Bloom's before twelve mildly curious onlookers, were a couple of appearances at independent bookstores on the Oregon coast, namely at Cannon Beach and Newport. That was that. What did he sell? A dozen copies? He knew the royalties, if Ripov ever paid him, wouldn't cover the cost of the gas to drive to the Oregon Coast in their aging Toyota, not to mention the value of his time on a per hour basis, which amounted to nothing. He was beginning to lose hope.

Devra had reminded him that even if he didn't sell many copies of *Tracking Tenure*, he was raising his profile from being a totally unknown author to a small blip on the literary screen in Oregon. The published title helped his resume as an academic and might help him land a real, full time, tenure track teaching job, not just piecework, paid per course taught.

Luther hadn't heard from Ira Ripov in weeks and had been warned by pal Charlie at *Publishers' Journal* that publishers didn't like to be pestered by authors who expected instant riches. Today's mail from Ripov, addressed by hand in formal copperplate on an announcement-style envelope, was a welcome surprise which he held in suspense. "Do you think it's a royalty check?"

Devra rolled her eyes. Devra didn't wear makeup and was blessed with the flawless skin of a twelve year old. She was still wearing her uniform from the VA hospital where she was a professional vampire, the med techs' inside joke about doing hundreds of blood draws from the pale, withered arms of disabled vets, no take home samples, please. Eventually she hoped to complete her nurse's training at OHSU, Oregon Health Sciences University, and be an RN. "Doesn't look like it. Checks come in number ten envelopes with windows. This one is almost square, fancy paper, looks like an invitation."

It was.

The formal invitation was printed on cream colored stock with a ragged edge.

You are invited
**to attend the
First Annual Lollipop Awards Presentation
At the Miami Book Fair
August 10. Reception at 7:00 PM Dress casual.
Overnight accommodations on board
the M/Y Lollipop
Crab Cake Marina, Biscayne Bay, Miami, Florida
RSVP**

The invitation was a complete surprise. He had never heard of the M/Y Lollipop, M/Y presumably standing for Motor Yacht. If the return address on the envelope hadn't been "Ira Ripov, Publishing Co. Inc." the invitation would have been a mystery. The address was a Miami Florida post office box, not Crab Cake Marina.

Lollipop was a silly name for a yacht, except, of course, Shirley Temple had sung a song about the good ship Lollipop in one of those old black and white movie reruns he had watched one night when his head ached from grading interminable student papers. What did Ira Ripov Inc. have to do with a yacht named Lollipop, and what did an awards ceremony have to do with him? Surely his debut novel didn't deserve an award.

Fortunately there was an explanation in the form of a note slipped in with the invitation. It read, "Luther, dear boy *(comma, so personal, no colon! And since when was he a dear boy? Was Ripov trying to be cute or just putting him down?)* at the book fair in Miami we're going to have a booth and a panel just for my authors. This is a great venue for you to plug your book and I know you'll be able to make some good connections. I insist that you come. (Signed) Ira Ripov."

"It's a command performance." He had never met Ripov or the editor whose ruthless alterations forced him into two more drafts. But Luther could not forget the terms of the iron clad contract he'd signed with Ripov Publishing Co. He was responsible for all promotional expenses, was expected to travel when requested, etc. etc. He had agreed that Ripov would have first refusal on any subsequent book, prequal or sequel, half of all eventual movie, translation, or television rights. Not that some foreign country ever would have any interest in an academic novel set on a fictitious university campus. In case of a dispute he had to agree to binding arbitration, whatever that was.

Not only that, but Luther was bound by a non-disclosure agreement not to reveal the terms of the contract to anyone but his lawyer. He couldn't disclose what he had agreed to to anyone, though he of course went over the contract with Devra. Devra had a keen eye for fine print, especially in the instructions for medicines whose veterans were prescribed, the fine print that listed numerous side effects like "may cause diarrhea, constipation, dizziness, or hangnails." She wasn't a co-author, but as his wife could be recipient of all the royalties if he were run over by a Tri-met bus while riding his ten speed to the university.

Considering that he was contract bound to pay promotional expenses, he'd be stuck with the air fare to Miami. "Looks like I have to go. How am I supposed to afford a flight from Portland to Miami? My god." Visions of their meager savings and mounting credit card debt.

"Maybe he's picking up the tab."

"Not very likely. Ripov didn't even give me gas mileage for those trips to the coast."

"Look at it as an investment. You might meet someone famous."

"What should I do, collect autographs?"

Devra gave him a sympathetic kiss on the cheek to encourage him. "Maybe there's a cheap flight, a red eye."

He could smell VA laboratory on her uniform. At least there were no bloodstains on the sleeve.

Luther had never been to Florida and he didn't want to go. It wasn't only the money. All he knew about Miami was the TV series "Miami Vice" which sounded dangerous. Wasn't Miami full of Cuban exiles, drug dealers, and retired New York Jews eating early bird specials?

Yet the thought of being aboard a handsome yacht, if the picture on the invitation were authentic, intrigued him.

Curious, Luther Googled the motor yacht Lollipop and there it was, an entry in a catalog of classic motor yachts. Originally christened the America, the yacht had been renamed by a later owner. Now the Lollipop, it was designed by Hyram Fischer, was 140 feet long, had teak decks and twin engines, cabins for a dozen guests, and a grand piano. It had been built in 1928 for a woolen magnate, a Horace Van der Gelder, who had not owned it long enough to enjoy it much before the 1929 market crash. Van der Gelder had gone bankrupt. The yacht languished for years, had been chartered by the US Navy for submarine patrol in World War II, but after the war had lain almost derelict until it was rescued in the 1970's by a dot com millionaire who restored it in 1930s period fashion only to be caught in the burst dot com bubble.

There were also photos of a grand dining room, an enclosed lounge big enough for dancing, and the grand piano. There was nothing in the entry about the current owner. Did Ira Ripov charter the good ship Lollipop? Own it? If so, he shouldn't be so stingy with the gas money for a book signing in Cannon Beach. Maybe Ripov was only boat sitting for the current owner who was away somewhere slaving away to earn the mooring fees.

Such a yacht had a history. Who knew what stories might come out of it, what had gone on below those teak decks, what famous people had coupled in the cabins below?

"Alright, honey. You persuaded me."

"Just don't bring me back one of those live baby alligators."

"They don't sell them anymore," Luther said. "People got tired of them, flushed them down the toilet. Now those alligators live in the New York sewers eating rats and bodies dumped by the Mafia."

"Who else do you think will be there?"

"Let's check the Ripov catalog." Luther fired up his Apple laptop and found the publisher's web site, something he had failed to do before. There was a list of books and authors. It was a mixed bag that showed an attempt by Ira Ripov to hit a broad spectrum of the market, not just be a niche publisher.

On examination beyond the titles of the books and their blurbs, the names of the authors were, well, startling. They were all names of famous, but dead authors. Was this a primarily reprint house, like Dover? Was Ripov publishing long lost manuscripts, or were the authors using pseudonyms to cash in on the reputations of the past and deceased? He knew there was a magician who called himself William Shakespeare, and a scientist named after George Washington, but this? It was improbable and bizarre, but there it was.

Besides Luther's academic novel, Ripov had published a collection called *Love Poems* by someone called Elizabeth B.B. then there was a volume called *Safari!* by someone named Ernest H--, something that looked like a business book called *Cubicle Chronicles* by a Franz K--, and a whaling history by a Herman M--. There was even something with a blurb suggesting it was science fiction, *Monster*, by Mary S-- and a horror called *Vampire* by Bram S--. There were others all over the spectrum of publishing. Surely those weren't the authors' real names.

Was this part of the Ripov business plan? A gimmick to draw attention? The variety of topics showed that his was not a niche, like someone who published only cookbooks or historical books. Or was he doing a shotgun blast at the market hoping something might hit?

Of course, if you wanted to call yourself William Shakespeare you could do that. William Shakespeare wasn't a copyrighted name or even a trade mark, but it could be confusing if you took on the pseudonym George Washington. George Washington Carver was legitimate, of course, but Herman M--? Ira Ripov's stable of authors had to be a menagerie of oddball characters. That sounded intriguing. What sort of person was attracted to whaling? Would the author of a vampire book bite?

"At least they're not a bunch of erotica writers," Devra commented. "I wouldn't want you to be spending nights on a luxury yacht with a bunch of horny bimbos with laptops and X-rated fantasies."

Now that was a thought. Not that he intended to be unfaithful, but he did look at the pretty girls in his classes and always kept his office door open if one of them came to see him. He had heard about girls who raised their GPAs by coming on to their professors. Then again, you never knew what accusations might be thrown if you didn't raise a grade.

Luther thought of a quip about horny interns at the VA hospital but decided he didn't want to go there. Devra might exercise her expertise at drawing blood at the VA to drain his veins for spite.

Being intrigued at the prospect of a junket on a yacht wasn't enough to pay for a ticket. Needing advice, Luther phoned Charlie Broadbottom at *Publishers' Journal* to tell him about the invitation for the Lollipop Awards ceremony.

Charlie sensed a scoop. "Tell you what, Luther, how about if *Publishers' Journal* gives you the assignment to do the story? Five hundred bucks, pending acceptance and on publication, of course, but it could cover that air fare."

"That would be great," Luther said, the anxiety draining out of him.

"But do it on the QT," Charlie warned. "Your publisher shouldn't know you're covering the event. You have a legitimate invitation. You don't need a press credential to get on board that yacht and you might find out more if people don't realize what you're up to. I've heard about that Ira Ripov. He's not a nice guy. You might end up at the bottom of Biscayne Bay in a cement overcoat."

"You're scaring me off," Luther complained. Did binding arbitration include agreeing to be stuffed in a barrel alive while concrete was curing around your legs?

"Just be your natural, relaxed, Midwestern self."

"You mean pretend to be a yokel."

"Put it this way. You're not in Iowa anymore."

"Thanks."

"You have a camera? Yet some digital pictures you can send me as attachments. Oh, one more thing," Charlie warned. "Have you paid attention to the weather channel?"

"No." Luther remembered that Charlie Broadbottom was one of those weather junkies who watched the weather reports. The Local on the 8's wasn't enough for him. Charlie loved those storm stories, clips of tornadoes, blizzards, and rooftops being blown away.

"This is hurricane season. They're already up to Greta, which is moving through Haiti and headed for Florida. Better pack your raincoat, wellies, and life jacket."

"Thanks a lot."

Luther didn't own a pair of what the British called "wellies," Welllingtons, high rubber boots. Oregonians never bothered with anything but good shoes. The students at Portland State wore flip flops all winter. He did have a good rain jacket with a hood, essential on his bicycle, but hadn't worn it since the rainy season ended in May.

With the prospect of the expenses paid, Luther made a reservation for the night flight to Miami . He sent an email to Ira Ripov announcing the itinerary and was told he would be met at the airport. Ripov would send a car for him.

At least there was no need to carry a box of his books as he had done in the trunk of the Toyota on those trips to the coast. Ripov would have an ample supply for the Miami book fair. He could manage with one carryon.

Ever mindful of his appearance, Devra packed the best of his two sport jackets, matching slacks and a single necktie, a couple of dress shirts and the rain jacket. In case there was a chance to lay out on the deck of the Lollipop in the Florida sun, Luther added an expensive six ounce tube of #30 sunscreen, his seldom used bathing suit and a pair of flip-flops. The Apple laptop and cord with the transformer added extra weight. All fit into the carryon with room to spare for some Florida souvenir. Devra had to have some compensation for not being able to go along.

Two

The red eye flight landed at Miami International Airport at seven-thirty in the morning and disgorged a motley assortment of bleary-eyed businessmen needing a shave, a quick wash-up and coffee before hurrying to an early meeting. There were a few weary National Guardsmen home on leave and still wearing their desert cammies. Mercifully, the babies carried by three young mothers had slept quietly through the night.

It was irritating that Homeland Security had confiscated the expensive tube of sunscreen because it was more than three ounces, so Luther would have to buy another. Damn.

As soon as he got to the Miami terminal Luther flipped open his cell phone and dialed home. It was too early for Devra to be awake, of course, being in the Pacific time zone, but their answering machine would pick up after three rings. He heard his own recorded voice saying to leave a message. "Hi, honey. I've arrived OK in Miami. Catch you later. Love you."

He wondered if Ira Ripov were going to meet the plane. How early would he have to get up in order to drive to the airport from Crab Cake Marina?

At the exit from the secure area he spotted a tall man holding up a piece of recycled cardboard with "Luther S--" scrawled on it. Could this be his publisher? Didn't seem likely.

Dragging the wheeled carryon, Luther walked up to him. "Ira Ripov?"

The man didn't look like the publisher of a book of romantic poetry though he might had served in a vampire thriller. He was dark-skinned, over six feet tall, skinny, with a scar on his left cheek that pulled his mouth into a sinister sneer like Dick Cheney. He was wearing scruffy khaki cargo shorts and a tight Tee shirt emblazoned with "Cuba si, Castro no." His one word answer was "Yesus." That was how he pronounced it. Spelled it was "Jesus," of course.

Jesus looked like some villain in a Miami crime series. Cuban, Luther realized. *He doesn't look like a Jesus to me, unless maybe one by el Greco, all stretched out and full of the anguish at being crucified.* Certainly Jesus was not a happy man.

Jesus took Luther's bag by the side handle and carried it like it was no heavier than a briefcase.

Luther followed his bag out of the terminal and into the parking garage. He was immediately hit by the Florida August humidity. Portland, Oregon had rainy winters and hot summers, but it was not what Floridians call buggy and muggy. It took your breath away. Almost stifled, Luther regretted that, thinking mainly of the formal nature of the awards business and the book fair, he hadn't packed any shorts.

The air was still as if Miami was holding its breath in dreadful anticipation. The sun was up but barely visible as a ghostly orb burning through a gray overcast. Was that Greta on the horizon?

Jesus didn't lead Luther to a limo or even a late model Cadillac that might be appropriate to a motor yacht's land transportation. There was a time when the vehicle of choice for California surfers was a convertible "woodie" with real wood on the doors. The Ripov wagon was the next generation, not real wood, but painted to look like it. The

Florida salt air had done its work. Rust was eating the station wagon like mould on cheese left too long in the back of the refrigerator.

The shocks were gone, too, as evidenced by the first spine-jarring bump as Jesus coaxed the wagon out of the airport and onto the freeway in the direction of Biscayne Bay. The windows were open letting in the roar of the muffler or lack of. Jesus turned on the radio, filling the car with Spanish music. Clearly, Luther had arrived in another world. What was he getting into?

Nervous, Luther asked, "Have the other authors arrived?"

Either Jesus didn't hear him, didn't understand, or preferred not to answer.

Resigned, Luther sat back and looked at the scenery, marveled at the palm trees, and wished that the wagon had air conditioning.

He took out his digital camera for a souvenir picture, but the bouncing wagon made it impossible to focus.

South Miami is not your beach front luxury of Miami Beach with its tall hotels, condos, and art deco mementos of early days. It's a neighborhood of walled yards, barred windows, and concertina wire. Biscayne Bay, which had once been filled with myriads of fish, had long since been polluted. It smelled stagnant.

The neighborhood of Crab Cake Marina was run down and seedy. Fenced parking lots were full of abandoned boats parked on trailers or up on blocks. The boats were bleached by the sun and stained by the rains, canvas covers rotted and hanging. The storage lots looked like the graveyards of forgotten dreams and dashed hopes. There were a few "For Sale" signs posted. Those looked like they had been there a long time without any offers.

There were one or two shacks advertising live bait and dating from the days when there were still lots of fish in Biscayne Bay. They passed a seedy looking bar, the Port O' Call,

The sign for Crab Cake Marina had seen better days. Marina was a misnomer. There was only one dock. The marina office was little more than a shack at the entrance with a barely legible faded sign at the side, "showers for boaters only". A ramp with a hand rail led down to a long, rickety floating dock tethered to tired pilings, each with its resident hungry seagull perched on top. One bird, Luther realized, was a pelican, its long beak tucked in as it snoozed atop a piling. He had never seen a pelican before. *Ugly bird.* A couple of water-filled derelict dinghies were tied alongside in the shallow water. Beyond them lay the M/Y Lollipop.

There she was, the name "Lollipop Miami" emblazoned on her stern in fancy gilt-edged letters. Just like in the invitation picture, she was dressed for a parade, gaudy signal flags rigged from the top of the mast to bow and stern. Luther didn't know what the flags stood for or if they spelled out anything, but the special ensign flown from the yardarm needed no translation. It was a golden lollipop.

No question, but the yacht was big. Clearly the picture on the invitation had been taken in better days. It was no longer a gleaming luxury yacht. The good ship Lollipop needed paint, polish, and varnish. The topside paint was streaked with rust where water had run down from the scuppers. On close examination, the signal flags were dirty and faded, had lost their initial gayety. The vessel had a small, but noticeable list to starboard.

Careful not to trip over the fresh water hose and the heavy, yellow power cord that led from the electric box on the dock and over the gunwale to the sockets on the boat,

Luther followed Jesus to the short plank that bridged the gap between dock and deck.

Before he saw his host Luther heard a voice from inside the cabin calling, "Ah, there you are, dear boy!"

Ira Ripov emerged, wiping his hands on a greasy rag.

Ripov was short, barely five feet, with a full, white beard that circled his face like a lion's mane. His head was topped with a gaudy, white Captain's cap, the bill decorated with lots of gold braid, what navy folks called scrambled eggs. Dark finger marks soiled the edge of the cap.

Ripov's blue eyes were bright and beady. With the beard they gave him the look of an alert wild animal uncertain whether to run for it or to attack. Ripov's face was deeply tanned by the Florida sun. His short sleeved designer shirt was open at the collar.

If it weren't for the clothes and the hat, Ripov could have passed for one of those derelicts Luther often saw begging on the streets of Portland, homeless, scruffy old men pushing all their worldly goods on stolen grocery carts. Ripov might have qualified as a gnome extra in some Hollywood Hobbit movie. He tossed the rag onto a bench, extended his hand. "Luther S--. Welcome aboard. Glad you could make it. Just call me Ira. Jesus will show you to your cabin." Jesus, not Yesus. "Be sure to sign the guest book."

"Guest book?" It was open on a little stand just inside the spacious cabin.

"For the IRS," Ripov explained. Was there a hint of sheepishness in his comment? Or did he have other reasons besides taxes? If Ira Ripov wanted an author's autograph he already hat the important one--on the bottom line of that nefarious contract. "Can't make this business deduction without a log ."

Made sense. The guest book was really a clipboard with a printed heading at the top starting with words in large print, "Welcome aboard the M/Y Lollipop" and followed by a paragraph of small print Luther couldn't make out. One didn't only provide a signature, but a printed name also and the date of arrival. The date of departure was blank, of course. His was the fourth signature, after Ernest H--, Bram S--, and Franz K-- who were already on board. But there were more authors on the Ripov web site. How many were coming? And which had opted out for reasons of health, prior engagements, or whatever?

Signing seemed harmless enough, just like any other guest book, though Ripov typically turned everything into a legal document. Luther dutifully printed his name and signed, making it official. He had arrived.

Three

So far Jesus had been so silent that Luther wondered if the man spoke English or was deaf or merely sullen and resentful. The only word he had said was when he identified himself at the airport as Yesus.

Carrying Luther's bag, Jesus led the way. The cabins were all below decks, entered by a stairway leading down from what had been a sumptuous lounge with the grand piano he had seen in the historic pictures found on the WEB. The curtains were faded by the Florida sun and the upholstered chairs were stained, perhaps by drinks spilled during a historic party on board.

Stepping uncertainly down a few steps and careful not to bump his head on the overhead, Luther found himself in a surprisingly long companionway with doors on each side. It was not unlike a European rail car, except in this case the Lollipop was beamy enough to have compartments on both sides.

All the doors were louvered for ventilation and had a high threshold one had to step over to get inside. Each had a tarnished brass holder with a slot for a card with the occupant's name. Luther's was on the starboard side, next door to Mary S--. The door was stuck. With a grunt, Jesus pushed it open, set Luther's bag on the floor inside, nodded, and left.

Though the Lollipop had the charm of the 1930's, the quarters down below lacked air conditioning. His was a small cabin with a porthole and a distinct smell of mildew. The narrow bunk was alongside the outer wall. Kneeling on the bed, Luther unscrewed the latches that held the porthole window shut, swung it aside in the hopes of airing out the cabin. There was no screen.

The compartment walls and ceiling were dark, varnished mahogany. Had they been painted white it might not have seemed so small. A chest of drawers was built in beside the foot of the bed with a mirror above it. Luther's reflection in it was tarnished. He saw that he needed a shave but his fresh haircut, a fifteen minute job at Quick Clips across from the university, looked OK.

The only hope for ventilation, aside from louvers in the door and the porthole, was an antique electric fan mounted above the mirror. Luther turned it on and it came to life with a rattle that settled down into a hum but brought little relief from the stifling humidity. He could imagine that on a muggy night it would be hard to sleep.

He unpacked. The minimum closet with three rusty wire hangers provided space for him to stow his sport coat and rain jacket. The rest went into the bureau drawers.

There was no sink. He'd have to find the bathroom. What did navy men call it? The head? Surely not on this vessel. The navy term came from the olden days when to relieve yourself you had to hang your butt over the side at the bow, which in foul weather might mean getting sluiced by a wave, the old salt's version of a bidet.

Luther took one of the two rather threadbare towels that had been folded on the bureau and, carrying his shaving kit, checked the other cabin doors. Ira Ripov had thoughtfully put name cards on all of them. Bram's came first on the

starboard side, Mary S-- beside Bram, then Luther. Ernest H-
- was across the companionway followed by Herman M--
and so on through the whole stable of authors in the Ripov
catalog. At the end the brass letters W.C. indicated he had
found what he was looking for. There were two bathrooms
on opposite sides of the corridor but the one on the starboard
side had a sign, "out of order." The door to the port side
bathroom was locked.

"Out in a second," a voice called gruffly from inside. The
door opened showing a broad face with a newly trimmed
beard and a tanned forehead. "Hi. I'm Ernest. Who are you?"

"Luther S--."

"You're the new guy."

Luther hadn't slept on the plane and was jet lagged.
Stifling a yawn, he ventured, "I guess. Last time I checked
my passport, anyway."

Ernest H-- emerged, his hairless chest bare. He had the
paunch of a man who drank too much. He wore a pair of
khaki Bermuda length shorts. He was barefoot. "Careful of
the hot water when you shave. It's intermittent. I think it's the
pump or the water heater or something. One minute you can
hardly get a trickle, then it gushes out scalding."

"Thanks for the warning."

"You just fly in, I take it."

"Yeh."

"You sign Ripov's guest book?"

"Doesn't everybody?"

"After you've freshened up go up top to the dining room
and find Maria. She's the Haitian cook. She'll fix you some
breakfast. There's just Maria and Jesus as crew."

"That's all? For a boat this size? No engineer or captain,
or such?"

Ernest gave him a hoarse laugh. "Ripov's too cheap. What use is there for a captain for a ship that never leaves the dock?"

"I guess not."

"After breakfast, come on down to my cabin. I've got some fine bourbon."

"Maybe later," Luther said. His fantasies about an offshore cruise faded. The yachting rule was the bigger the boat, the less time it left the dock. The Lollipop must be a permanent fixture. Besides, if Ripov was too cheap to have more than a crew of two, how would he pay for fuel for the twin engines Luther had read about on the Internet? The ship was probably doing double duty as office, home, entertainment center, and guest hotel, all deductible.

Four

In the dining room, which Luther recognized from the photo on the Internet, a dark-skinned, skinny girl in a maid's apron was checking the coffee urn on the buffet. She was wearing a thin, cotton dress and looked undernourished. Her black hair was pulled back into a knot. She had the tired look of someone who worked long hours for little pay. That must be Maria, the Haitian cook and maid.

In Portland the menial jobs taken by new immigrants were filled by Mexicans, Russians, and Africans. In Florida it must be Cubans and Haitians.

Maria saw Luther, said nothing, but indicated with a wave of her hand and a nod of her head that breakfast was ready. Maybe, like Jesus, she had little English. Then she disappeared into the adjoining galley.

Breakfast was laid out on the buffet under heavy silver-plated covers which on inspection proved to be scrambled eggs, hash browns, and something that looked like broiled fish. A loaf of Win-Dixie sliced white bread, still in its plastic wrapper, was placed beside a do-it-yourself electric toaster. The butter was slowly sagging in the heat on a dish beside.

There was already someone at the long dining room table, a small, dark-haired man with a coarse black beard, tousled hair, and, in spite of the Florida heat, a jacket of a

European cut, complete with waistcoat and a dress shirt with an ascot tie.

"Morning," Luther said as he set his plate and cup down at the place opposite.

"Morgen," came the answer. "I am Franz."

"Luther S--. I'm the author of *Tracking Tenure*."

"Stupid title for a book," Franz K-- commented.

"Blame the editor. You wrote, what was it? *Cubicles*, right?"

"*Inside ze Cubicles*."

"Did you choose that title, or did Ira Ripov's editor force it upon you?"

Franz was clearly offended. "I choose my own titles."

Luther wasn't looking for an argument. Maybe Franz K-- wasn't a morning person. "This your first time in Florida?"

"Ja. *Furchtbar*. I hate it."

"I haven't seen enough to make up my mind," Luther said. So far what he had seen was seedy and run down. Whatever Florida had promised in the way of an American tropical paradise in the 1920's when the Miami art deco buildings had gone up had been spoiled by developers, the Great Depression, and the ravages of sun, humidity, and hurricanes. "What's so bad about Florida?"

"Cockroaches. If you read your entomology you zee zat Florida is ze home of ze American cockroach."

"I never took biology," Luther admitted.

Franz was having trouble pronouncing his th's. "Here zey call zem Palmetto bugs. Zis big." He held up his fingers, spread about three inches. "Did you bring with you any Raid? Bug spray?"

"No." Luther hadn't seen any signs of cockroaches when he put his clothes in the bureau drawers. Maybe he should have been warned, but even if he had been prepared, airport security would have confiscated a can of Raid along with his sunscreen. If he'd known he'd have asked Jesus to stop somewhere to pick some up.

Franz glowered menacingly across the table under thick eyebrows. "Ze Palmetto bugs fly. Don't leave your porthole open at night. Zey are everywhere."

Luther was tempted to look under his plate. Franz obviously had a thing about cockroaches. "Do they bite?"

"Zey eat anything, even ze bindings of books. Sometimes you can get ze feeling zat you can turn into a cockroach yourself," Franz said with a shiver of disgust.

"Sounds like a good idea for a book," Luther said. "What sort of books do you write?" *Inside the Cubicles* could be about anything. Office politics, maybe.

"Various things. Ze law. And you?"

"I'm just a beginner," Luther admitted.

Franz nodded bitterly. "If I didn't have a job in insurance I'd be K.O. Royalties from Ripov? Ha! Don't kvit your day job."

Luther admitted it was good advice. He'd seen no royalties, not a penny from his book. According to that contract he was supposed to get quarterly reports. None had come. It didn't sound like Ira Ripov was very forthcoming with payments to authors.

The talk of cockroaches dampened his appetite. He turned his attention to his scrambled eggs, breaking the yellow mass into very small pieces in case a Palmetto bug had got into the pan and committed suicide. He changed the subject. "Have you met Ernest?"

Franz nodded. "A madman. He has a gun."

"A pistol?"

Franz had lifted his coffee cup to his lips and almost chuckled. "You see for yourself. He vill show you. He shows everyone."

The guests aboard the Lollipop were proving to a menagerie, indeed. So far the host looked like a gnome, Jesus like some Cuban assassin who no doubt hid a switchblade in the pocket of his shorts, Franz who was obsessed with cockroaches, and Ernest who drank whisky in the morning and carried some sort of a firearm. What next?

Luther wasn't in a hurry to accept Ernest's offer of an early morning drink. He finished his coffee, left his plate and the cup where Maria could pick them up, and left the Lollipop dining room.

Ira Ripov seemed to have disappeared.

Ira had not explored the ship. He knew from the Internet historic photos that there was a lavishly furnished master stateroom but those furnishings were probably long gone. Perhaps Ripov had turned it into an office for his publishing company.

Remembering his assignment from *Publishers' Journal*, Luther took his camera, went out onto the covered deck to take a few pictures. He had to walk to the very end of the dock to get a bow-on photo of the Lollipop, backing up as far as he could without falling into the cove.

A whisper of wind rippled the waters and he could smell rain. The overcast had taken on a dark, menacing look. With the sun gone it looked more like late afternoon or early evening. The pelican that had roosted on one of the pilings had disappeared. The seagulls, ever watchful, seemed nervous. Good think he'd packed his cycling rain jacket.

He heard the now familiar rumble of the company station wagon's leaky muffler. At the end of the dock Luther saw that Jesus had returned, presumably from another airport run, with another guest. Who was it this time?

Jesus opened the rear door for his passenger. What emerged was a small man who got out of the station wagon. The new arrival blinked and sniffed the air like a ground hog emerging from its den and blinded by the light.

Jesus opened the back of the wagon and removed a duffel bag and what looked like a case for a fishing rod.

Luther didn't fish. In Portland had had thought about fishing for salmon or steelhead in the Willamette river, but when he and Devra bicycled the riverfront path he was turned off by the signs that said, "In rainy conditions, do not come into contact with this water." If the river was so polluted that mere contact with it could be infectious, he wanted no part of any fish he might catch.

He walked down from the end of the dock to greet the new arrival. The newcomer wore thick eyeglasses and walked with his head down, a posture of permanent defeat.

Before Luther could reach the short gangplank and the gap in the Lollipop's railing he was intercepted by Ira Ripov who called, "Herman! Dear boy. Glad you could make it."

This must be Herman M-- author of the whale book....

Ripov acknowledged Luther's presence and introduced them. "Herman, this is Luther S--, one of our authors."

The narrow dock was not a good place for a conversation. Followed by Jesus with the duffel bag and long rod case, they came aboard. "Be sure to sign the guest book," Ripov said before leading the way to the aft lounge.

Squinting at the fine print but unable to read it, Herman M-- signed.

When new, the aft lounge, though covered, would have been open, but it had windows and was screened against mosquitoes and the ominous palmetto bugs that Franz K-- had warned about.

"You two get acquainted," Ripov said. "I've some work to do." Again he disappeared, waddling on his short legs.

Jesus put down Herman M--'s baggage and left.

"Going fishing?" Luther asked. "Looks like you came equipped."

"Ah," was the brief reply. Herman was dressed in a faded, loose shirt that could double as a jacket. The cuffs were frayed. The double breast pockets had unbuttoned flaps. Herman drew a cigar from one of them, took a clip and a box of matches from the other breast pocket, snipped the end of the cigar, then lit it with a match he struck against his leather shoe sole. The match, shaken, was deposited in an ash tray he'd discovered on a side table. He took a long, satisfying pull on the cigar. It was a theatrical ritual done for Luther's benefit. Only after it was completed did Herman M-- reach for the long, tubular case.

It didn't hold a fishing rod. Instead, with the loving care reserved for museum treasures, Herman took out a long, pointed instrument.

Luther recognized the pivoting tip. It was meant to penetrate, then rotate so it couldn't pull out. "A harpoon? I don't think you'll find any whales in Biscayne Bay."

"Shark, maybe. They feed at night, you know. Hang a lantern over the side, throw in some fish guts, and wait. Never know. Might get lucky."

Luther couldn't imagine what one would do with a shark if he caught one. Ernest, down below in his cabin with his whiskey and gun, Franz with his obsession with cockroaches, and now Herman with a harpoon. What next?

"The cabins are down below. I'll show you." He picked up the duffel bag, which proved to be heavy, perhaps with books. "Careful on the steps. They're steep."

"I had hoped the Lollipop was a sailing vessel," Herman complained. "Life is full of disappointments." He looked like a man who had suffered many.

The Lollipop had one mast, but it seemed to have no other function than to hold a radio antenna and decorative signal flags, not a sail. "Maybe Ripov publishing will change things for you."

Following Luther down the steep stairs, Herman commented. "If not, there's always the possibility of mutiny."

"Mutiny?" Luther had heard about mutiny at sea, but never on a ship that apparently never left the dock.

"Mutiny is a last resort. I have been in a mutiny."

"Really?" But Herman did not elaborate.

Luther found Herman's cabin. "If you haven't had breakfast, it's laid out up in the dining room. Scrambled eggs, coffee. I've got some pictures to take."

"Got to be careful about pictures of famous authors," Herman warned. "Never publish without a release."

Had Herman guessed Luther was secretly doing a story for *Publishers' Journal*? Surely not. But then, more than one person might have an assignment to cover the story of the Lollipop Award. There were other magazines, *People* for instance, or *National Inquirer*. With so many prestigious authors on board at one time, there was probably a story. The *Sun,* only a step above the outrageous *News of the World*, was published not far away in Boca Raton. That was the grocery tabloid that did the bat boy and alien baby stories. It would likely publish "Whale harpooned in Biscayne Bay." Anything to sell papers.

Five

With a rush brought on by a full belly, Luther's jet lag and exhaustion from a sleepless night on the plane caught up with him. Even though it was still morning he had to get some Z's. Back in his cabin he discovered he had forgotten to turn off the little electric fan. There was no improvement. The air was still stifling.

The only light came from the twelve inch, open porthole.

Taking off his shoes, he lay down in the bed under the porthole and tried to sleep. The Lollipop lay as steady as if it were parked on land. Except for the nautical layout, the small cabin might as well have been a room in a budget motel. Well, not even that. Even the cheapest motel had a color TV. The cabin aboard the Lollipop didn't even have a clock radio.

He closed his eyes and became aware of the sounds of the old yacht. Somewhere down below he heard a quiet hammering. What was it, the compressor for a refrigerator? Too distinct for that. There was no air conditioner, at least not for this part of the boat. He knew from the thick yellow cord on the dock that the Lollipop had shore power, so it wouldn't be a diesel generator. The sound was not constant, but intermittent. Some kind of a pump, he reasoned.

What was it, a bilge pump? He didn't notice any hoses that might have carried the yacht's waste water to a sewer on land. When the Lollipop was built they probably didn't have holding tanks for the waste water, and simply dumped it into the sea. If that were the case, no wonder Biscayne Bay was so polluted.

In the days before water treatment plants, the myth was that the solution to pollution was dilution. Of course, that didn't work. God only knew what crap was pouring from all those yachts and ships into Biscayne Bay. If he hung over the railing with a lantern at night, Herman M-- was unlikely to harpoon any sharks.

Luther closed his eyes and tried to sleep. He thought he heard rustling in the closet. Could that be those cockroaches eating his only jacket? No. They wouldn't eat nylon, cotton, or polyester. Maybe, besides palmetto bugs, the Lollipop had ship rats or mice. The thought was not conducive to restful sleep.

In spite of the strange sounds, Luther fell into a drugged-like stupor.

He awoke to a clap of thunder and rain on his face. Sitting up, he had to quickly swing the porthole shut and dog down the screws that held it tight against the weather. The old glass was scratched with age, but he could make out sheets of rain hammering the waters of the bay. Was hurricane Greta coming closer?

Though not a weather junky like Charlie Broadbottom, he remembered from the frequent reports on the TV that hurricanes were preceded by bands of heavy rains and squalls, even tornadoes. Was this one of those, or just a quick, tropical downpour that would be over in a few minutes only to dry out and turn into 100% Florida humidity?

Luther put on his shoes, got his yellow cycling rain jacket out of the closet, put his digital camera in the pocket and went upstairs to the covered side deck. As he came up there was a flash of light, an instant clap of thunder, and the smell of ozone. He remembered the Lollipop's mast. Anything sticking up could act as a lighting rod. Had the ship been struck? Sounded close enough.

Pelted by the rain, a yellow taxi pulled up beside the marina office shack. The passenger door opened and a hand came out, holding an umbrella. Once it was opened from inside, a woman got out. Bare legs showed under the three quarter length blue rain coat.

The driver popped the trunk from inside, rolled down the window to collect the fare, but did not get out to unload the woman's baggage. She had to get it herself. Two bags, one large, wheeled, the other a small carryon.

Two bags and one wind battered umbrella were more than a handful, so Luther hurried up the steep ramp to help her.

The rain hammered on the hood of his yellow jacket.

The power pole beside the Crab Cake marina office shack had a big, gray transformer at the top. A blinding, tremendous crack of blue-white lighting struck the power pole. The transformer blew apart, showering sparks like the Fourth of July.

Not waiting to close the trunk, the cab driver sped away in a panic.

"Better get out of here," Luther shouted to the woman as he grabbed her bag.

She took the smaller one. "Isn't it wonderful?" she asked, beaming out from under her umbrella.

"What?" What was wonderful about nearly being struck by lightning in a Florida cloudburst?

"The power of nature," she shouted.

"Watch your step," Luther warned as they made their way down the railed ramp to the dock. The tide was out, the ramp down to the floating dock at its steepest angle.

The power was out. There was no longer any light in the Crab Cake marina office and not on board the Lollipop.

Luther heard someone running up above. Ira Ripov was shouting, "Jesus! Get down below and start that generator."

The tall Cuban appeared from someplace forward and, carrying a flashlight, brushed past Luther. He must have been out deck in the rain, for his Cuba Si, Castro No shirt was soaked.

Jesus-- chauffeur and engineer, too?

There was a fierce gust of wind and the Lollipop actually shifted at the dock, the fenders creaking. The floating dock rocked against the pilings. At this state of the tide the pilings stuck up about ten feet above the deck. What if Greta brought a twelve foot storm surge? Would everything simply float away? Or was Biscayne Bay sufficiently protected, not like New Orleans in Katrina?

"Welcome to Florida," Luther said. "I'm Luther S--. And you are""

"Mary S--."

"Oh, the author of *Monster*."

"That's me."

She was pretty and young but already had the look of what was called "a woman of a certain age," a woman of sensuality and sexual maturity. Luther wondered if he could look her up on his laptop computer. Amazon.com night have a brief bio of this well-known author along with her book. Maybe the Wikipedia had something about Mary S--.

"Ira Ripov wants everyone to sign the guest book. Something about taxes."

There was another crash of thunder, but the center of the storm was moving away. Already the rain, though heavy, was less intense. The storm would probably be over as quickly as it started.

He was glad the Lollipop wasn't his yacht and that he was not out on the bay in some little fishing boat. If a hurricane hit, what did people do with their boats? He'd heard that the safest place for a navy ship in a hurricane was well out at sea, but even at 140 feet, the Lollipop seemed hardly capable of weathering a storm at sea.

Luther had seen pictures of yachts and fishing trawlers swept up on land and piled like toys along the shore. Shouldn't Ira Ripov be thinking of evacuating? Sending his stable of authors back to pasture? And what about the Miami book fair? Would it be cancelled, or did people tough it out come hell or hurricane?

The companionway down below was dark. "Your cabin is down below next to mine," he said, leading the way. "Put your hand on my shoulder. I'll lead the way." He must remember to buy a flashlight. They made slow progress, a step at a time. Mary S-- held onto him tightly, afraid to stumble. It was like descending into an unlit cellar. Once her cabin door was open there'd be light from the porthole. "Watch your step."

Mary S-- stumbled and held onto him for support. It was almost an embrace, a grasp that she didn't release right away when they got off the bottom step. He had offered his shoulder, hadn't expected a hug.

There was a rumble from somewhat aft and below. The lights in the companionway flickered, then came on. Jesus had done his job quickly.

"Ah, that's better. Jesus got the generator going."

"Jesus?"

"The Cuban driver and jack of all trades."

Mary asked, "Who else is here?"

"You mean crew? Just Maria, the cook and maid."

"I mean the other authors for the awards ceremony."

"Herman M-- just arrived. Then there's Franz K-- and Ernest H--. No sign yet of Bram S-- and there must be some others yet to come."

"Should be interesting. No other women?"

"A poet," Luther said. He couldn't remember her name. Was it Elizabeth B--, the author of the love poems?

"Sounds like a nice party," Mary S-- said. "I love a party, sitting beside the fire and making up stories."

"No fireplace on board," Luther said. "Here's your cabin. Mine is next door." He pushed open the door for her. "The bathroom's at the end of the hall on the right. There are two but one's out of order. There's lots out of order on this ship. It's old, you know. Built in about 1930."

"Does it have any ghosts?"

Luther hadn't thought of that. Of course, an author of a book called *Monster* probably had a thing for ghosts, just like Franz K-- had a thing about cockroaches. "I don't know. Maybe you can make one up."

About to close the door behind her, she gave him a look that might have been flirtatious. "Maybe I will."

Six

The near intimacy with Mary S-- made him nervous. His instinct as a happily married man was to flee. Luther was ready to take Ernest H-- up on that drink. He knocked at the cabin door and found the author standing up at the built-in bureau. He was typing on a portable manual typewriter, an old machine that looked like it had been through the wars. Ernest had removed the top of the battered carrying case which stood on the floor.

No touch typist, Ernest pecked away rapidly with two fingers, the mark of a seasoned newspaper journalist in the days before computers.

"What, no laptop?"

Ernest shook his head. "I hate computers. No use out in the bush when you're on safari."

"I guess not."

"Tried them.," Ernest continued. "Keys too small. Hit the wrong one and you've lost a day's work."

"Got to remember to save the file every few minutes." At Portland State almost every student had a laptop computer. They used them in his class. In the hallways at the student union students could be found everywhere there was a wall socket they could plug into. "What is that, an Underwood?"

"Same make used by Ernie Pyle in the Pacific."

Luther didn't remember who Ernie Pyle was. "You always write standing up?"

"Old back injury. Can't very well have this thing on my lap. No room in here for a chair."

"Herman M-- has arrived. Imagine--he carries a harpoon. Says he can use it for shark spearing from the deck."

Ernest wrinkled his forehead in amazement. "Hardly the right equipment for Florida. He'd need a rod with steel leader and at least fifty pound test line."

"You a fisherman, too?"

"Fished off Cuba before the revolution. Marlin. Bill fish."

The most Luther had ever caught were a few bluegills in a pond back in the Midwest. "You didn't bring a fishing rod. Franz K-- says you have a gun."

"Yep." Ernest motioned to a large plastic case standing in the corner. It was locked. "I'll show you." He wore the key on a chain around his neck, lifted it over his head, and unlocked the gun case. He removed a heavy, double-barreled rifle which he held in both hands with loving care. "That's my baby. Elephant gun. Can stop a rhino in its tracks. Used it in Africa before my accident. You better brace yourself when you fire this beauty. Recoil will knock you on your ass." It looked like a cannon.

"Wow. No elephants in Florida. Biggest animals around here would be manatees and nobody would want to shoot one of those harmless creatures. What could you possibly use this thing for?"

"Book tour prop," Ernest explained. "I'm the author of *Safari* and other adventure books. Like the ad says, 'Don't leave home without it.' "

That explained the rifle. It must be risky to take an elephant gun on board a plane. Of course, he couldn't take it as a carryon, but could baggage handlers be trusted not to steal it?

"You mentioned a drink."

"Any time," Ernest said. "Got a bottle right here."

"I'm not much for whiskey," Luther said. "What about a beer? There must be some on board. We could ask Maria."

Ernest shook his head. "If we asked Maria to rustle up a couple of bottles of beer Ira Ripov would probably charge us for it. He's that cheap. We can find a bar someplace. Let's go."

Luther remembered seeing a bar on the way to the yacht.

Ernest had a raincoat in his closet but by the time they emerged on deck the cloudburst had ended.

"We can ask at the marina office," Ernest said, leading the way.

A utility truck with a mounted cherry picker hoist had already arrived to replace the blown out transformer.

"That was quick," Luther commented. "The power company is on the ball."

"They must get plenty of practice around here."

The marina manager and a helper were mounting plywood over the windows of the marina office. The manager was a middle-aged, paunchy man wearing a Dolphins baseball cap. His assistant, like Jesus, was a Cuban pushing a battery-powered electric drill as they screwed the plywood to the window frame.

"We're looking for a bar," Ernest explained.

"What's the matter? Old Ripov out of booze?"

"Ernest here is afraid Ripov would charge us for a beer."

The manager nodded. "He would. The bastard owes me for three months mooring fees. I'm not saying anything for now. If he holds out long enough I'm putting a lien on the Lollipop. Would make a great party boat."

Luther remembered the out of order sign on the second bathroom. "Considering the condition, I think it would cost a fortune to restore it."

"You've got a point there," the manager said, and handed his helper a couple of screws. "Every eight inches, now. We don't want this to blow away."

"What about that bar?"

"Just up the road. It's called Port O' Call. Nice place. Good crab cakes."

Ernest squinted his eyes. "Is it clean? Well lighted? I like a clean, well lighted place."

"They sweep the floor at least once a month," the manager said, and turned back to the preparations for Greta.

Luther didn't think cleanliness would be an obsession for someone who went on safari. Luther didn't know anything about hunting expeditions. Didn't people stay in tents? How did they shower?

Crab Cake Road had no sidewalks. The two men picked their way around the puddles, had to duck when a pickup truck splashed by pulling a boat trailer. Those who could were taking their boats out, not that being parked would prevent them from blowing away if Greta actually struck. When Hurricane Andrew hit south Florida the only thing left of some houses were the concrete slabs they'd been built on.

The Port O' Call, unlike the other establishments on Crab Cake Road, while old and weather-beaten, showed an effort at being spruced up, no doubt to cater to the boaters and fishermen who had money. It was, to Ernest's satisfaction, well lighted and if the floor weren't swept often, the tables were clean.

A stuffed sword fish was mounted on the wall above the bar. Such decorations can be bought made of plastic without the necessity of skinning a real fish. A rusty, antique gaff and fishing rod were also mounted on the wall along with some old-fashioned lures with large hooks. Bits of retired fishing nets were draped around the walls to complete the nautical effect.

Ernest sat briefly on one of the bar stools, winced because of his back, and stood instead.

The bar maid was a chesty woman wearing a tee shirt stenciled with "Boaters do it on the water," but the last three words were under the curve of her bosom and hard to read.

"Seen enough?" she said, conscious of Luther staring at her tits.

"Just reading your shirt," Luther said, embarrassed. "You have Coors?"

"Sure. Glass or bottle?"

"Glass, please."

She turned to Ernest. "And you, mister?"

"Jack Daniels on the rocks."

"Man after my heart." She served them up. "You come down to fish? I can tell by your accents you're not local."

If Luther's ear was accurate, she wasn't local, either. She sounded or like a transplant from Australia or New Zealand, one of those travelers who overstayed their budget and had to stay on to work.

"We're authors."

"Authors! What do you write?"

Ernest sipped his whisky. "Novels, short stories, articles. Used go write for newspapers."

"I've just got one novel," Luther said apologetically. Beside Ernest H-- he felt like a rank amateur.

"I'm going to write a novel some day," the barmaid said.

"Better get busy," Ernest said with a weary tone as he leaned against the bar. "Everybody's ahead of you."

"So what are you down here for? Fishing?"

"We're here for an awards deal and the Miami Book Fair." Luther explained. "Staying aboard the good ship Lollipop."

"That wreck? I'm surprised it's still afloat."

Ernest swirled the ice cubes in his glass. "If it stays at the dock there's no danger."

"It's only for a couple of days," Luther explained.

"Must cost you plenty," the barmaid said.

"We're guests," Luther said. "It's a business trip."

"Uh huh." She was plainly skeptical.

"You know the owner?"

"Ira Ripov, the bearded Hobbit? I sure do. He owes me for six cases of beer."

Luther's dreams of royalty checks were looking like a pipe dream. If Ira Ripov didn't pay his mooring fees and stiffed the barmaid for cases of beer, he could easily fudge the sales reports of his book. What did they call it in California? Hollywood bookkeeping? By the time they paid for the caterers and the psychiatrists for the trained dogs there was nothing left.

That was a sobering thought. Luther was glad Charlie Broadbottom had given him an assignment that would pay for the red eye flight. From the sound of it, he was likely to get billed for being picked up by Jesus at the airport.

Ernest made a fist, cracked his knuckles. "In Africa on safari someone like that could easily have an accident."

"You mean, finding a snake in his bed?"

Ernest nodded. "Or meeting a jackal on the way to the latrine the middle of the night."

"Florida doesn't have jackals," Luther said.

"It has alligators."

The barmaid was listening. "Not in Biscayne Bay, but since Castro sent a bunch of prisoners over on the Mario boat lift, we have more than enough monsters on the loose. The first language of this part of Florida is Spanish."

Caught up in the thought of Cuban criminals roaming the streets, Luther said, "I wouldn't want to mess with Jesus. Mr. Ripov better pay that guy on time. He looks creepy."

"It's an act," Ernest said. "Like they say in the ghetto, Jesus has a attitude."

Luther poured the last of his bottle of beer into his glass. "Could have fooled me."

A Dade County police car pulled up outside the Port O' Call and an African-American uniformed deputy got out. He wore suspenders to hold up the pounds of gear attached to his belt-- gun, handcuffs, radio, stick, and something that looked like it held a spare clip of ammunition, or maybe a phaser. The policeman was broad shouldered and narrow waisted, didn't need any of that gear to command respect. He gave Ernest and Luther a quick assessment then sat down at the bar next to them.   He took off his cap, revealing a shaved head, and set it on the stool beside him. "Hi, Sally. Coffee. Some storm."

"Power was out for awhile."

"Lucky the Lollipop has a generator," Luther said.

The cop was interested. "You fellas from the Lollipop?"

"Just guests," Luther said. "We're here for the so-called Lollipop Awards ceremony."

"What the heck is that? Old Ira Ripov handing out candy?"

"Beats me," Ernest said.

"Some kind of literary award Ripov cooked up. You know Ripov?"

Sally the barmaid poured coffee for the policeman.

He opened one of those little packets of Half and Half and stirred it into his cup. "That crook? Behind those beady eyes and shit-eating grin is the heart of a weasel. I bet he called you 'dear boy.' "

Luther remembered the words of the note that came with the invitation. "Come to think of it, he did."

Ernest turned to the deputy. "I don't suppose you're writing a novel, too."

"Nope. Screen play."

Ernest chuckled and turned to Luther. "What did I tell you? Everybody's doing it."

Police had a reputation for expecting free stuff from tradesmen on their beat, so it was a surprise to Luther when the cop put down a crumpled dollar and change for the coffee. "Thanks, Sally." To no one in particular he said, "If Ripov ends up in the bay nobody will miss him." He set his cap back on his head and saluted with two fingers. "See yah."

"There's a thought," Ernest said with a wink. "Maybe if Ripov welches on the royalties we can threaten to pitch him overboard."

"I hope you're joking."

"Has he paid you anything?"

"Not so far," Luther admitted.

They paid for their drinks and started to leave the bar. Luther asked Sally, "Any place I can buy a flashlight?"

"There's a bait shop further up the road. Might have one."

Luther remembered her name. "Thanks Sally. And about that novel you're maybe going to write some day. Don't quit your day job."

The two men walked together, dodging the puddles and the traffic. They found the bait shop. Besides tanks containing live shrimp and minnows, displays of fishing lures and other gear, they found a couple of made in China flashlights. Luther bought one that was waterproof and a couple of batteries. Who knew when the power on the Lollipop would go out again?

Cautious not to reveal the details of his contract with Ira Ripov Publishing, Luther asked Ernest , "Did you have to sign a non-disclosure agreement?"

"I told him to stuff it," Ernest said. "Remember, Luther, all contracts are negotiable. Ripov is bluff and bluster. Little guys like to be dictators. Did you know Napoleon was only about five feet tall? They like to lord it over other people."

"Or put others down."

"You mean like that 'dear boy' stuff. It's only one step away from calling that black deputy 'boy.' Not any more you don't. "

The sun was breaking through the overcast as they walked back to the Crab Cake Marina. The horizon, however, was still dark and threatening.

All the windows of the marina office were now secure. Most of the slips were now empty as boat owners removed them from harm's way. Owners of the remaining, larger boats were securing them to the pilings with extra lines. Absentee owners whose boats were tied to mooring buoys offshore might be out of luck.

Jesus was securing the Lollipop with extra spring lines to prevent the boat from surging back and forth in a swell. He looked up as Luther and Ernest approached. Never talkative, his one word greeting was "Lunch," with a motion of his head.

"I wonder if everyone's here." Luther reviewed the roster of names he had seen on the cabins of the Lollipop. "I guess we're still missing that poet and Bram S--."

"Oh, he's already on board," Ernest explained. "Came in last night."

"He wasn't at breakfast."

"He's a funny guy. Stays in his cabin. I think he's identifying too much with the characters in his books."

"Oh?"

"Didn't you know? He wrote *Vampire*."

"I forgot. What does he do, sleep in a coffin?"

Ernest shook his head. "Beats me. Maybe he won't show up until after dark. He chuckled. "You should see him. I bet Ira Ripov wouldn't call Bram his dear boy."

They both laughed.

Luther, wondering what Bram S-- must look like, shook his head. Authors. Strange people, these authors. Why did they use pseudonyms instead of their real names? Maybe their real names were boring or embarrassing, like Jack Schitt. It struck Luther as all an act. Kinky Friedman, the Texas Jewboy, had cultivated a bizarre persona complete with cowboy hat, leather jacket and cigar. Had Tiny Tim deliberately created that goofy hair style and look, or was he the real thing? And was Mary S-- really Mary S-- or someone else? It was confusing.

Luther wondered what people thought of him. He was, well, normal. Whatever that was. He wrote under his own name. Maybe he should create for himself a persona. Herman had his harpoon, Ernest his elephant gun. What did the author of an academic novel carry? Chalk?

Ira Ripov greeted them as they came aboard. "Been checking out the neighborhood, boys?"

Ernest ignored the slight.

"Bought a flashlight," Luther said and held up his purchase.

"Good idea. I've asked everyone to meet together at lunch so we can make plans for the book fair."

"I hope the contract for your booth has a provision for a refund of the fee in case the show is cancelled," Ernest said, a dig at Ripov's penchant for fine print. Or maybe the book fair would turn into a hurricane party.

"Paid with a credit card," Ira said through his white beard. "I can always dispute the bill. Lunch in half an hour."

Seven

Half an hour gave time for Luther to hang up his rain jacket and fire up his Apple laptop

Coming aboard the elderly yacht was like traveling through time. He didn't find a wall socket in his tiny compartment where he could plug in the power cord. The restoration of the Lollipop hadn't included 110 volt wiring to the guest cabins. In 1930 laptop computers and electric hair dryers and shavers hadn't been invented. Once the battery discharged he would have to hunt for a power source. In the meantime--what?

He had not yet started his report for *Publishers' Journal* and didn't know where to begin. He created a new file and put down notes. Something about the yacht. Something about Ira Ripov Publishing. Something about the bearded man Sally the barmaid had called a hobbit. And then the authors.

He would have to be careful. If he wrote what he thought about them he could be sued for libel. Luther knew nothing about libel law, but he did know that if he and Devra couldn't afford to rent anything larger than a studio apartment, they surely had no place in their budget for lawyer's fees. He would have to be careful.

The safest thing would be to start with a description of the Lollipop. If it weren't actually afloat it might be described as a derelict, even a ghost ship. Mary S-- had asked if there were any ghosts.

Maybe at some time or other there might have been a murder on board. A yacht that old and that big had to have a hidden history, intrigue, romances, conflicts. There was nothing about anything like that in the Wikipedia, just some bare facts.

Charlie Broadbottom had been vague about this assignment. Did he want a thousand words? Five hundred? Or did the publication have space for something in depth? Luther decided he'd better use the old inverted pyramid style of newspaper writing and divide the story into sections so the editors could cut out whatever they didn't have space for.

One thing was sure: he didn't want anyone aboard to guess what he was doing.

After sketching a rough outline he shut down the laptop. If someone were curious, they couldn't get past the password he had set up in case some student tried to sneak a peek at his files when he left the classroom. He stowed the laptop in the top bureau drawer, changed out of the clothes he'd spent the night in on the plane to Miami, and went up for the command lunch.

The table in the Lollipop's grand dining room could seat twelve. It retained that antique look, old fashioned furniture that had survived the period when the Lollipop had been used by the Coast Guard in World War II. Perhaps the chairs had been stored in a warehouse to preserve them for postwar restoration.

To Luther's surprise, he noticed that even the tableware was antique. The handles of the spoons and forks were monogrammed. The initial was not an L for Lollipop, but an A. Luther remembered the yacht had first been named America. Van der Gelder, the original builder, had been an immigrant from Holland and no doubt wanted to show his pride in making it in his adopted country. It was lavish.

Ira Ripov wasn't. If he could stiff the local bar for cases of beer and not pay his mooring fees (not to mention royalties for his authors), what would lunch be like?

Luther had half suspected that Ripov would serve them hot dogs or sandwiches on paper plates with plastic forks. Not so. He noted the number of forks--three, which might mean an appetizer, salad, main course. The little spoon set across the top promised a possible ice cream dessert. The usual coffee cup, a water glass and a beer glass completed the setting. It promised to be an elaborate lunch, not just a sandwich.

Franz K--, biting his lip, was waiting pensively in the corner of the dining room. He was still wearing that foreign-looking jacket, but had discarded the vest. The ascot tie was gone, too. Franz was succumbing to the Florida heat. Perhaps, like some victim of the tropics in a Conrad novel, Franz would deteriorate into a rum-guzzling decadent in soiled white linen. Not that he was likely to find any free rum aboard Ripov's boat.

Mary S-- came in. She had changed from her traveling slacks to a cool-looking cotton blouse and a tight skirt so short she would have to be careful to sit with her knees together. All Luther knew about her was the title of her book. He didn't know if she were married, single, or lesbian. He deduced that if she were married she wouldn't dress like that.

Luther was married, but that didn't mean he couldn't look at an attractive woman and speculate. "Hi," he said. "All settled in? Cabin OK? No ghosts?"

She arched an eyebrow. "Not yet. But I heard something rustling in the closet."

"Palmetto bugs. That's what Franz K-- says the Floridians call them. Cockroaches. He's obsessed by them. He hates bugs."

"He needs a couple of wolf spiders," she said. "They thrive on roaches. If there's time maybe I can catch him a couple."

"Do wolf spiders bite?"

"Not people, but you don't want to handle them."

Luther got Franz K--'s attention. "Franz! This is Mary S--. She says she can catch you some wolf spiders to hunt down those bugs."

Franz K-- stood up with a barely perceptible bow. "Zat would be good. *Sehr gut.*"

Ernest H-- arrived. He had ditched the khaki cargo shorts for a pair of rumpled slacks and a short sleeved shirt only partly buttoned to show his manly chest.

They all stood around uncomfortably, waiting for Ira Ripov before they sat down at the table.

Their host finally appeared, still wearing his silly captain's cap. He led a trophy blonde in a red power suit open at the neck showing cleavage. "Boys and girl," Ira Ripov began. "Let me introduce Caroline, my assistant. She'll be helping out with the booth at the book fair. She's the one who sees to it that all your books are displayed properly. Caroline is your coordinator. Anything you need, ask her."

Clearly if Ira Ripov were going to hire an assistant it wasn't going to be some elderly biddy. If he were going to hire somebody, if she were a sexy blonde with boobs, all the better. Ripov looked like a man with no qualms about exploiting his female staff.

Luther didn't have an assistant. The department secretary was a nice girl. Messing with the university staff was trouble with a capital T.

Ira Ripov Publishing had to be more than a one man show, Luther understood, but until now he didn't have any idea, beyond the editor that had made him do so many changes and corrections, what sort of staff Ripov had. Maybe the editor, like the authors, worked on a contract, basis--piece work, one book at a time, no vacation time, no benefits, no income tax withholding, and probably no social security. That was what you could expect from Ripov. He was so tight he squeaked.

"Please, sit down, everybody. Maria has prepared a special Haitian lunch."

They sat. Ira, his white beard fairly glowing. He was still wearing that captain's cap-- or was it another? When Luther first saw him it was a soiled cap with lots of gold on the bill. This one was clean, no gold. Ripov must have a collection of them. "Wait a minute," Ripov said as he looked crossly around his table of authors. "Where's Bram?"

As if he'd planned a grand entrance, Bram S-- showed up at the door to the Lollipop's grand dining room. If Franz K-- could look uncomfortable, Bram, author of *Vampire*, looked like worry personified. His forehead was furrowed by perpetual wrinkles and his mouth turned down into a frown he would carry to his grave.

Except for the large, shining cross he wore on a chain around his, Bram S-- could have passed for an invisible man, the kind of person you'd never notice in a crowd. If his clothing had included a white, clergyman's collar he might have been mistaken for a priest.

Not only did he wear a large, shiny cross, but dangling on a leather thong around his neck was a little bag about the size of a golf ball. What did he carry in that? Some lucky charm, like a rabbit's foot?

Garlic, Luther guessed. If a Christian vampire repellant didn't work, Bram had a pagan backup. *The guy's so obsessed with his own vampire book that he's taking no chances. Maybe he thinks one of us might bite him on the neck. Now who could that be? Not me. Mary S--?* The thought made Luther laugh out loud, which, to his own embarrassment, drew everyone's attention.

Some cast of characters, Luther thought. It reminded him of the board game "Clue." What would it be? Jesus in the library with a knife? Maria in the kitchen with some Haitian voodoo curse? Colonel Saunders in the parlor with a poker? He could probably write a book about that. Must remember to work that into the notes on his Apple.

Then he remembered it had already been done, only the setting was a mansion and it was a movie, "The Rocky Horror Picture Show" with "incest is best." That wouldn't work on the Lollipop unless Caroline was Ira Ripov's daughter. Now there was a possibility. Had Ripov ever been married?

"There you are, dear boy," Ira Ripov said with a false smile that didn't reach his beady eyes. "Sit by me. It's safe."

Bram had a strange, high, Michael Jackson voice, as if his testicles had never dropped. "You sure you're safe sitting by me?"

Ernest whispered to Luther, "What a lot of shit. You catch that 'dear boy' routine?"

Luther didn't say anything.

The Lollipop's galley was adjoining and Jesus came in, no longer in the Cuba Si, Castro No tee shirt, but wearing a white waiter's jacket and a sullen expression. He carried a heavy tray which he set on the sideboard. He and Maria, in her white cook's apron, served the shrimp salads.

They ate. To Luther's disappointment, the main course was some sort of unidentified Haitian rice dish with vegetables and hot spices that made him quickly empty his glass of ice water. Had Ripov forgotten the beer? Those glasses remained untouched.

Herman M--, who had sat, subdued, ate only a few mouthfuls of the Haitian dish and pushed the plate away. Blinking through his thick eyeglasses, he commented, "Some fish would have been nice. Florida is known for its variety of fish, red fish, snapper, sea trout, grouper."

"Not too late," Luther said. "Maybe shark will be on the menu tomorrow. See if you can spear one with your harpoon."

"Or something," Herman said.

What did he mean by that?

If Ernest brought his elephant gun as a prop for the fair, maybe Herman's harpoon was just that, a theatrical prop for a reading from his book.

Luther caught Franz suspiciously searching his food for telltale signs of the feared Palmetto bug. If cockroaches were in the cabins, surely they must have headquarters in the galley, nesting under the stove, behind the refrigerator, in the cupboards. Unless you liked to eat bugs, it was enough to turn a person off his food completely.

Though the shore power had been out during the storm, the freezer hadn't lost its cold. The dessert was a small scoop of vanilla ice cream served in chilled silver cups monogrammed, like the tableware, with an elaborate A.

The coffee was thin. No doubt Maria has simply added more water to the breakfast grounds.

Lunch over, they got down to the business of the Miami Book Fair.

Eight

While Maria and Jesus cleared the dining room table Ira Ripov led the way up to the bridge of the Lollipop. The room aft of the bridge had been turned into an office. To Luther's relief, this one had air conditioning. It also had the usual--a computer, copier/fax/scanner, filing cabinets. As befit a company office, there were bookshelves under the closed windows with copies of all the books Ripov Publishing produced. Luther sought for and found a couple of copies of *Tracking Tenure*.

Behind the desk stood an antique safe that might or might not still be serviceable, providing Van der Gelder's combination to it had survived multiple owners and the many years the Lollipop had been out of service.

There were not enough chairs to go around, so Bram S-- and Luther used a low bookshelf for a bench. Ernest H--, obviously in some back pain, stood.

Ripov's assistant, Caroline, handed out brochures for the Miami book fair. It was to take place in the Victoria, a Miami Beach convention hotel. Luther noted that on the map of the convention hall the location of the Ripov booth was circled in red. Nice photos of the hotel and the swimming pool adjoining the sandy, Atlantic beach.

Luther wondered if he'd have time to change to his bathing suit and sneak away for a dip some time during what promised to be a long day.

Mary S-- had found the schedule of speakers. "We're not all here. Don't you have a poet on the list?"

"You mean Elizabeth B--," Ripov said. "She couldn't come. She's too ill to travel. At least that's her excuse."

Ira Ripov took his seat behind the desk. The desk had a green, banker's lamp and an antique-looking pen set. There was no in or out basket, just a single sheet of paper which Ripov consulted before speaking.

He began with the plan for the next day. "We'll all drive over to the fair tomorrow morning. Jesus will drive the station wagon and Caroline here will drive the van I've rented. The books have already been delivered from the warehouse in Miami and set up. You'll each take two hour turns at the booth for signings. There are panels for the different genres which will hold forth in the adjoining meeting rooms. You've all made public appearances before. The panels allow you ten minutes to give your spiel and there will be questions afterwards. Tomorrow I'll give you each your name tags that identify you as authors for Ripov Publishing. At the end of the day the banquet program has a slot for the Lollipop Awards ceremony. I expect the press will be there, so no cute props."

Ripov fixed his beady eyes on Ernest H-- and Herman M. 'By that I mean leave the harpoon and the elephant gun. They stay in the booth. Caroline will keep an eye on them for you."

Ripov sat up straight in his chair and stroked his copious beard, cleared his throat. "This book fair is important. If you've followed the trade reports you know the publishing business in this country is hard hit by the recession. For several years there has been consolidation so now there are only five major publishing houses left in the United States. Only one of those is American owned. All the rest are foreign.

"Not that consolidation has helped any. Thanks to new technology, so-called Print on Demand, anybody can call himself an author. We've gone from, thirty thousand titles published in a year, primarily non-fiction, to over three hundred thousand. Most of those books will never go anywhere. Many are unedited trash. The average sales of those titles are about three hundred copies. This is hopeless. The public has no idea what's a good book. The fact that daily newspapers are going out of business means there are fewer book reviews being published.

"You see what we're up against. Then there are the distributors. The distributor I deal with wants a 60% discount off the cover price. The bookstores get 40% but even then bookstores don't buy the books. They take them on consignment. They display them for a month or two and if they don't move the copies are sent back, shopworn and unsellable. The paperbacks have the covers torn off and returned for full credit. My investment in the printing is lost. When the book are actually sold, the distributor sits on the money and doesn't pay me for ninety days, sometimes longer. So if you haven't got your royalty checks, now you know why."

That was sobering news for Luther. He had hoped that his debut novel would make something to justify the two years he had worked on his book. Devra had reminded him that since it had served as the thesis for his creative writing degree at the University of Iowa he had, in a sense, already been paid for his labor. The degree displayed proudly on the wall of the office he shared with two other adjunct instructors didn't pay rent for a larger apartment. Why was he doing this? Would having published a novel give him brownie points toward a full time, tenure track position? That was the hope. If it worked, maybe it didn't matter if the book didn't sell.

Ripov wasn't finished. "Now boys and girl, before you all disappear for the afternoon, I want to speak with each of you privately on the bridge. Ernest, you first."

It was like being summoned to the principal's office. Luther felt talked down to. These were all seasoned, professional authors. They were used to speaking in public. They had done book tours. Ira Ripov's demeanor treated them as if he were the coach of a bunch of Little League baseball players.

Ernest H--, with a backward look at Luther, followed Ripov through the varnished, mahogany door onto the bridge. Brief glimpse of a ship's wheel, binnacle, and antique engine room telegraph.

The others sat nervously, looking at one another, wondering what was going on on the bridge.

Outside there was a rumble of thunder. The first sounds of rain ticked on the roof and spattered the windows. Pushing a sun-faded curtain aside, Luther looked out at the harbor. Not many boats remained at the dock and only a few swung on their moorings. The rest had been evacuated for safety.

It was the second band of rain storms circling around Greta. Had Charlie Broadbottom been there he could have given Luther a minute by minute account of the progress of the hurricane, whether it would simply douse Florida with rain and pass harmlessly offshore or turn and sweep its eye over Miami. Unfortunately, with no television weather channel to watch and no NOAH weather radio receiver, the only weather observation Luther could make was outside the window. If the Lollipop had wi-fi service he could have picked up the weather report and radar on his Apple. No such luck.

Luther counted the seconds between the lightning flashes and the thunder. Sound travels about a mile a second, giving him a rough idea of how close the squall line was. He guessed three miles. And how fast would the storm be traveling? Twenty miles an hour? He hoped the Lollipop's mast was grounded.

There were muffled sounds of an argument on the bridge and Ernest H-- emerged, steaming. "That son of a bitch." He turned to Luther. "He wants to see you next. Good luck, 'dear boy.'"

As befitting a captain, once on the bridge Ira Ripov had jammed his soiled yachting cap down on his forehead. He leaned against the antique ship's wheel and looked up at Luther who was a foot taller. "You're new to this business, Luther, but I expect you to get out there tomorrow and sell books. Not only your own, but the whole list. You may not be into Mary's monster book or Bram's quasi-scientific treatise on vampires, but you've got to put your heart into it."

Luther heard himself saying, "Yes, sir."

Ripov scratched his beard as if searching for his chin somewhere inside it. "If you don't sell books, Luther, Ripov Publishing won't survive and you won't get any royalties, understand? Nowadays publishers expect their authors to get out and beat the bushes. You won't see much advertising. You have a blog?"

Luther admitted he hadn't.

"On Facebook? Twitter?"

Luther shook his head. He was feeling more and more inadequate. "I'm working on a web page. Not done yet." It was a poor excuse. He had a hard enough job grading all those Portland State University student papers and preparing three different lectures. How could he fit in time to keep up a blog and all that internet madness? His impact wouldn't be more than one raindrop in the storm that was now pummeling the roof of the Lollipop's bridge.

He'd had the wrong idea about publishing, the wrong idea entirely. He thought authors got big advances, that publishers sent salesmen around. He had seen a few textbook drummers, new graduates with fresh-baked literature degrees, graduates who had jobs with New York publishing companies only to learn that they had to put in a year or two on the road. Those sales persons had come to his office at PSU, but they were peddling textbooks, not novels. Maybe he was writing the wrong stuff. He should be editing an anthology for Norton. Fiction… that was crap.

But Ernest H-- had done OK. He'd had a best seller and one of his books had been made into a movie. Luther's academic novel was baby stuff by comparison.

Luther waited while Ripov blew off steam. Hell, Ripov was just the publisher, not his boss. He couldn't be fired but Ripov acted like Luther was an employee. It was discouraging, but it made him angry, too. Maybe he was angry at himself for being such a chump, taken in by his own dreams of glory. This was hard reality.

He was angry at Ripov, too. Ira wanted everyone else to do all the work. He took advantage of hungry authors, made them sign iron clad contracts, then expected them to sell. It was easier to write a book than to sell one.

He thought about the notes he had thrown together on his Apple. This put a new slant on things. What would he write for *Publishers' Journal*?

Leaving the rest of the authors to do their turn in the barrel. Luther retreated despondently to his cabin. He shouldn't have made the trip to Florida. It was all a waste of time. No wonder Herman M-- had that look of permanent defeat, packing that phallic harpoon like Captain Queeg with his ball bearings. It was pitiful.

Sitting on his bunk and listening to the electric fan simply circulating the same damp, musty air, Luther thought about Herman M-- and the others. Herman had mentioned mutiny. When a ship's crew got discouraged and angry enough, they turned on the ship's officers. Maybe that's what Herman was hinting at. How would he react to Ira Ripov's demands. How would Franz K--?

If Ripov didn't play his cards right, his pep talk could backfire.

Nine

Luther heard the door to the cabin next door slam. The walls to the compartments were thin. In spite of the sound of the rain beating against the closed porthole and the hull, he heard sobbing next door. He knocked gently on the wall. "You OK?" he called. Obviously she was not.

Luther put the Apple into sleep mode and shut it. He knocked at Mary S--'s door.

"Come in." She was sitting in her bunk, there being no chair, and wiping her eyes with a tissue. "He's such a terrible man."

"He read you the riot act, too?"

"If he thinks science fantasy is passe, why did he buy my book?"

"He's just trying to intimidate you. Bullying is a poor management style."

She sniffled. Her mascara had run, but without her makeup she was still a beautiful woman.

If he'd been single Luther would have set on the bunk beside her to comfort her and maybe more. It was tempting, and she looked like she was available. He chose to stand in the open doorway. "Look at it this way," Luther said. "He might have had a casting couch." That was the Hollywood tactic. Actresses were forced to use sex to land parts in the movies. Did female authors have to do the same?

"I could deal with that," Mary S-- said. "My husband wouldn't have stood for it."

So, she was married. "I would hope not."

"He's dead, of course. Drowned."

"Sorry to hear that. How did it happen?"

"Small sailboat. Storm."

"Oh." Luther remembered his article assignment. He would need character sketches of all the principals to flesh out his report. "What exactly did Ripov want from you?"

"He expects me to vamp the customers. *Monster* isn't a romance and it's not erotica. It's about what it means to be a human being."

"I don't think Ripov knows what that is."

She got up, looked in the mirror, didn't like what she saw and daubed her face with a bit of cold cream which she then wiped off, removing the damaged makeup. "Ripov's a monster, all right. "

"He must have some redeeming qualities. He bought my book."

Mary S-- looked at him. "He wasn't helping you. He was helping himself. Did he pay you anything?"

"No, not yet."

"You think he's going to pay you anything at all-- ever?"

"Well, it's in the contract."

Mary S-- tossed her head, then fussed with her hair. "He's got that non-disclosure agreement. "We're not supposed to talk about our contracts."

"Hell with that. Maybe we should all compare notes," Luther suggested. "It would be what Herman calls a mutiny."

Mary thought about it. "In *Mutiny on the Bounty* the captain was put off the ship. The mutineers expected him to die at sea, but he didn't. The crew made it to a tropical island and eventually killed each other. The leader, Mr. Christian I think his name was, was hanged. I don't think I'm interested in that kind of mutiny."

Luther remember the extra dock lines Jesus was making fast. "The Lollipop's not at sea. Discussing your contract with fellow authors is not a hanging offense."

The yacht, large as it was, could come adrift. Larger ships than that had been swept ashore by hurricanes. How safe would they be on the Lollipop if Greta came ashore with winds over a hundred miles an hour? What if a storm surge lifted the floating dock over the tops of the pilings that held it in place? What then? Certainly they'd have all gone to some shelter long before that.

Mary S-- had another idea. "I think we should all figure out how we can get out of our contracts. Take our books to some other publisher."

"That would be a mutiny, all right. Maybe we should confront Ira Ripov and get him to add a codicil to our contracts giving us that option."

"That's a thought." She smiled. "No need to set him adrift in a life boat."

"We'll have to be quiet about it, though. If we disclose the contents of our contracts, he could sue all of us."

Luther remembered that somewhere in his contract was a clause about binding arbitration. He didn't know how that worked, but he suspected that Ira Ripov, if pressed, would want money from anyone who crossed him.

He'd talk to Ernest about it. Herman M-- would be game.

Ten

There was a cursing and a pounding in a compartment across the companionway. "What is it?" Luther shouted.

It was Franz K--. He had come down after his turn with Ira Ripov on the bridge deck and was stomping and kicking.

Mary S-- whispered, "I think he's having a tantrum."

Luther guessed that everyone had their own way of reacting to Ira Ripov. Mary S-- had cried in frustration and anger. Ernest had cursed. Now Franz was stomping and kicking.

They cautiously opened the louvered door to Franz K--'s cabin. The little man was stomping his feet and kicking. "*Verfluchte kakelaker*!" He noticed Luther and Mary S-- watching him. "Damned Palmetto insects. Cockroaches! Did you see it?"

Whatever it was it had disappeared somewhere, perhaps in the closet or under the bunk.

"No bug spray?" Luther asked. Luther didn't like cockroaches, either. The apartment he'd shared back in Iowa City with Charlie Broadbottom had been infested with them. It had been an endless battle of human wits versus an insect's survival instincts. The human might win an occasional battle, but in the end it was the roaches that survived.

"I told you you need a couple of wolf spiders," Mary said, and to Luther, "Do you have a flashlight?"

"I just bought one. I'll get it."

"Wait for me up on deck. I'll ask Maria for a couple of jars. We're going hunting."

"In the rain?"

"Get your jacket."

Puzzled, Luther put on his yellow cycling rain gear and went up onto the covered side deck.

The rain was steady now and heavy, a virtual monsoon, and the air was no longer still. A strong breeze was kicking up whitecaps in Crab Cake Cove and spray was splashing over the breakwater. The palm trees along the shore bent to the gusts of wind, their fronds swishing. The rigging leading to the Lollipop's mast hummed whipping the little signal flags. A couple of them had already gone to shreds. Outside the marina office the flag pole displayed a couple of little red flags. What was the Coast Guard code? One for a gale, two for a storm, three for a hurricane? What was the sustained wind speed? About forty, Luther guessed. Charlie Broadbottom the weather junkie would love this.

Still, the Lollipop was a good sized ship. She must have weathered many a storm since the 1930's including hurricane Andrew. Luther felt secure on board.

Mary S-- emerged from the galley with a couple of glass jars with lids. She had put on her blue raincoat, but the umbrella would have been useless in the wind. "Let's go."

"Where?"

"That storage shed next to the marina office."

Luther hadn't paid any attention to it before. It had a corrugated metal roof. Unlike the marina office whose windows had been covered with plywood in preparation for the storm, the windows of the storage shed were unprotected.

They had to pick their way carefully on the rain slick dock. The tide was up, and the ramp not as steep as it had been. Luther's feet were already wet.

The marina manager was locking up his office. Luther said, "I'm Luther S-- and this is Mary, an amateur entomologist and one of Ira Ripov's authors. Do you mind if Mary and I check your storage shed for wolf spiders?"

"Wolf spiders? Never heard of them."

"They hunt cockroaches," Mary explained. "The Lollipop has roaches."

"Doesn't everybody in Florida? Help yourself."

The door to the storage shed was ajar. Though the noise of the rain on the metal roof forced them to shout, inside it was dry and musty. A couple of old outboard motors, partly disassembled, lay off to one side. There were coils of rope, a pile of fishing nets, stacks of used lumber.

"This is a perfect place," Mary said. "Over here. Hold one of these jars. Get ready with your flashlight."

"You've obviously done this before," Luther commented.

The roof rattled. One corner was loose. If the wind got much stronger the entire roof would probably blow away. It was not a good place to be if the whole place collapsed.

"Gotcha!" Mary exclaimed with triumph. She clapped the lid on the first jar and held it close to Luther's face.

He turned the flashlight on the jar. Inside was a fierce looking spider with a wolf like face. He wouldn't want to tangle with that one.

"They're harmless unless you're a cockroach," Mary said. "Hold this and give me the other jar."

They switched jars. Luther made sure the lid he now held was on tight. "If I had to choose between cockroaches and one of these rascals, I think I'd take the cockroach."

"They only hunt at night," Mary said as she crouched beside the stack of used lumber.

In no time she had found another.

"I suppose you couldn't put two in the same jar," Luther commented. "They're eat each other."

Another gust of wind shook the storage shed. The roof was definitely coming loose. "Let's get back to the Lollipop," Mary said. "This place is going to blow away any minute."

"How'd you explain to Maria that you wanted a couple of empty jars? Use sign language?"

She looked at him and wrinkled her nose. She pushed rain wet hair out of her eyes. "I speak French, silly. Spent winters in the south of France. Used to go sailing on the Med."

No sooner had they closed the door to the storage shed behind them than the wind blew it open again. There was a crash as an eight foot palm frond, blown loose from one of the trees, crashed through one of the shed windows.

Careful not to drop the jars with their quarry, they clung to the railing of the ramp down to the dock. Though stable before, the articulated sections rose and fell with the swells that were building in the cove as the seas hooked around the breakwater.

Once in the shelter of the Lollipop's covered deck, Mary proudly held up her catch. "Aren't they beautiful?"

"Not my idea of a pet," Luther said. "So you were able to talk to Maria. She's Haitian, right?"

"She's also illegal," Mary said. "Ira Ripov gave her a job off the books. She doesn't like the job or him but has to work for him or he'll hand her over to immigration."

"But he pays her, doesn't he?"

"I wouldn't be so sure of that. She's got a bunk in the crew's quarters. There's a couple of cabins at the stern above the engine room. She's on one side, Jesus on the other."

"Is Jesus an illegal, too?"

"I think so," Mary S-- said. "The two of them are virtual slaves on board."

Luther had read about foreign diplomats who kept servants as maids, paid them only room and board, no social security or workman's comp, no tax withholding. There had been some scandals about that. Even prospective White House appointees had to be rejected because they hadn't paid social security for their domestic help. No wonder Jesus had that sullen expression. If he and Maria weren't paid enough for a bus ticket out of Miami, they were stuck between Ira Ripov and the INS. Not a happy crew.

"Let's see what Franz thinks about his new pets."

Franz K-- cringed when he saw the pair of wolf spiders. Always with a worried expression on his face, he looked like he was ready to stand on his bunk to put distance between himself and the spiders.

"Not to worry," Mary reassured him. She opened his closet door, unscrewed the cap of the first jar, and the spider disappeared in the dark interior. "Just make sure he's not sleeping in your shoe when you put them on. Don't want to kill the poor thing."

She pulled out the lower drawer of Franz K--'s bureau, revealing a cozy place the dreaded palmetto bugs could nest. "Off you go, spidey," Mary said, and carefully replaced the drawer. "If any palmetto bugs come into this cabin they're in for a surprise."

"*Danke*. Thank you," Franz said, though from his tone of voice he didn't seem so certain.

With the three of them in the compartment there was barely room to turn around. They emerged, Mary with the two empty jars, Luther in his rain jacket with flashlight.

They were met in the companionway by Herman M-- who straightened up, surprised, blinking at them through his thick glasses. "You're all wet. Been out in the storm?"

"Hunting spiders," Luther said with a shiver. "Nasty buggers. Speaking of nasty buggers, how did you make out with Ira Ripov?"

"I'll tell you in a minute." Herman looked to both sides. Though the doors to the compartments provided some privacy, they were not sound proof. "Not out here."

Herman led the way up to the spacious aft lounge. There was no one else there. The old windows rattled in the wind. There were puddles on the deck, rain water that had found its way through the casements. One corner of the carpet was already wet.

Since the two jars had already served their purpose, Mary placed them under a window where they could catch some of the drips.

Luther, Mary and Herman sat in a close circle on the lee side of the lounge. The rain hammering the roof was so noisy that they had to keep their heads close in order to hear the conversation.

"Ripov expects us to do all the work for him. Then there's that award he mentioned in the invitation. You got one, too, I assume."

"The Lollipop award," Luther said. "What is it, some kind of trophy?" Maybe it was no more than a computer generated certificate, suitable for framing, but of no consequence.

"A publicity stunt. He's got it on the schedule for the book fair. Presumably one of us is going to get the award, whatever that might be, so the news releases will boost one of our books."

"Not a bad idea," Luther said.

Herman shook his head. "Not bad if what you want is to get us all competing against one another. Divide and conquer."

Mary nodded. "I see what you mean."

"Have any of you talked to Bram about this?" Luther asked. He wanted to interview Bram S-- for his article anyway. This would give him the opportunity. "If not, I'll sound him out. See what he thinks. Ernest is already steamed."

Mary agreed. "You do that. I've got to change out of these wet clothes. This raincoat is advertised as shower resistant, not like your jacket."

Luther's jacket didn't keep his pants dry. Walking the short distance from the Lollipop to the shore and back was enough to get him soaked below the hips.

"See you at dinner," Herman said. "I think I'll go sharpen my harpoon."

Back down in his compartment, Luther changed into his other pair of slacks, got out his laptop and returned to the draft of his article for *Publishers' Journal*. During a lull in the storm he was again conscious of the sound of some sort of motor down below. If it was a bilge pump, was the Lollipop leaking? An old yacht like that must have plenty of places like the windows in the lounge where rain water could penetrate. What about the decks?

He decided to explore the yacht and see where the sound was coming from.

Eleven

At the aft end of the companionway beyond the bathrooms was a steel, water tight door. Luther opened it and found a short passage with a door on each side, which he guessed were to the crew's quarters. To one side a ladder led down to the engine room. That's where the noise was coming from.

Twin diesel engines with an array of wires and pipes dominated the space. Instead of a solid floor around them there was a grating, sections that could be lifted out to gain access to the bilge. One of the gratings had been lifted up on its hinges. The noise was coming from down there.

Luther trained his flashlight down into the space and saw water. Then he heard someone sloshing about. "Who's there?"

The beam of a flashlight danced around. Jesus emerged, his face smeared with oil. He could not stand up in the low space. He looked worried.

"Are we sinking?"

Jesus's head bobbled. "No sink." But he didn't sound convincing. "Pump OK."

"But there water down there."

"Always some water. Old boat."

"So you always have to keep pumping? What if the power goes out?"

Jesus stood up straight in the opening and hoisted himself out of the bilge space. He pointed to a piece of machinery mounted beside one of the big engines. The engines had not been wiped clean and had a look of disuse. The equipment Jesus indicated was in running order. "Generator."

That must be what he started up when the transformer was struck by lightning and they lost shore power.

Jesus gestured to Luther that he should get out of the engine room.

Luther climbed the ladder. He wanted to talk to Jesus about Ira Ripov, but didn't know if the Cuban knew enough English to speak in whole sentences. "Does Mr. Ripov pay you?"

"No pay." He gestured toward one of the crew cabins. "Sleep here."

"Ripov is supposed to pay you," Luther explained. "He's supposed to withhold taxes and social security."

Jesus didn't understand taxes or social security. Obviously he wouldn't grasp workman's compensation, either.

"He's a bastard," Luther said. "Ripov bastard."

That was a word similar to Spanish. "*Bastardo*," Jesus said, and drew his finger across his throat.

"Why don't you just quit?"

"Immigration."

The statistics bandied about in the press claimed there were seven million illegal immigrants in the united States, but most of those came from Mexico. There were other central and south Americans, too, people from Honduras and Columbia, wherever there was unrest and poverty. In Florida the illegals were Cubans and Haitians. Some were desperate enough to set off in rafts of truck inner tubes lashed together. Many drowned. If intercepted at sea, the Coast Guard sent them back, but if they made it ashore they were entitled to some sort of legal process before they were deported. With the INS case load overwhelmed, that could take years.

No wonder there were illegal immigrants who stayed long enough to have babies in the United States, children who were then US citizens by birth, but might have to be separated from their parents by deportation.

Luther thought, *It's none of my business. I'm not going to denounce Jesus and Maria to immigration. The one who should get it in the neck is Ira Ripov.* Luther shook his head sadly. "Too bad." He put on a sympathetic expression and held out his hand. "OK?"

Jesus understood the gesture. They shook on it. "OK. *Si.*"

Jesus might look sinister, but his attitude was of a man exploited and resentful. Luther would not want him for an enemy.

Luther returned to the guests' section of the Lollipop and went looking for Bram. If he was not in his compartment, where had that guy with the cross around his neck and bag of garlic hidden himself?

Luther heard a piano, followed the sound, and found Bram S-- in the ship's lounge. The old grand piano was the same Luther had seen pictured on the internet series of historic photos of the Lollipop. The lounge was well appointed with a bar. Bram was picking out what Luther recognized as an Irish tune. The dampness on board a yacht in Florida's humidity was not a good place for a piano. It was out of tune, making the melody Bram was playing hard to recognize.

"Been looking for you," Luther said when Bram noticed him standing beside him at the piano.

"Quite a rain. Reminds me of Dublin."

"It's the fringes of hurricane Greta," Luther explained. "So far it's just squalls, but if the hurricane comes ashore we'll probably have to evacuate."

Bram stopped playing. "Aye, if that happens they will surely cancel the book fair."

"Then we'd have made the trip here for nothing," Luther said. "Except for the so-called Lollipop award. If it's only given to one of Ripov's own authors it can't have much national weight."

Bram nodded. "There are awards and awards. Same as reviews. A review in some small town paper is useless. Sure if you're not reviewed in the New York times you've naught to be bragging about."

"What about your book, *Vampire*? How's it doing?"

"Making a bit of a splash."

"Earning any money?"

Bram turned to Luther. "Not a shilling. I fear our dear leprechaun of a publisher is keeping his pot of gold to himself."

"Something has to be done about that," Luther said. "Nobody else has been paid, either. We're entitled to an audit, aren't we?"

"That's in my contract," Bram admitted, "but we're not supposed to discuss those details."

"We could if we all got together and hired an auditor."

Bram held up the glittering cross he wore on the chain around his neck. "What we need is my vampire to suck the blood out of him. Or at least scare the bejeezus out of him."

Luther shook his head. "Ripov is a crusty guy. I don't think he scares easily."

"I wouldn't be so sure. Notice he never takes off his captain's hat?"

"Maybe that's his lucky hat," Luther suggested. "You think he's superstitious?"

Bram gave Luther an evil grin. "The curse of the Irish upon him then."

They were interrupted by the tinkle of Luther's cell phone. He thought it might be Devra calling, but the screen said "unknown caller." "Hello?"

"There you are, Luther. How are you enjoying the hurricane?" It was Charlie Broadbottom in New York.

"So far it's lots of rain and some gusty wind."

"I wish I could be there with you. I've been watching the weather channel. It looks like Greta is going to give Miami a pass, heading out to sea."

"That's a relief. I was afraid the Good Ship Lollipop would sink at the dock."

"How are you coming with that article for me?"

"Just an outline so far. The authors are all upset with Ira Ripov the publisher. He gave us a sob story about the nature of the book business."

"I'm familiar with that. Everybody's crying. Everybody's writing books, but nobody reads books anymore."

"Ripov owes money to everybody, hasn't even paid his marina fees. Stiffed the local bar for cases of beer. So he expects us to all sell a ton of books and get him off the hook."

"Lots of luck, old buddy. I'd like to see you on the best seller list."

"Not a chance," Luther admitted. "I'll send you what I've got as an email attachment and you can have a look at it, let me know how to proceed. What's the deadline?"

Broadbottom laughed. "The usual. Yesterday."

Nothing like motivating people with anxiety and stress, Luther thought. Teaching those large classes with all that paper grading at Portland State could be stultifying, but if he didn't get papers done on time, he was to some extent his own boss. He could be late and not fired. "I'll have more to write after the fair tomorrow."

"OK, Luther. Too bad about your missing the hurricane."

Luther shut the cell phone and put it back in his pocket. As if Charlie Broadbottom had some control of the weather, the rain suddenly slacked off. Maybe they were being spared after all.

"What was that about?" Bram asked.

"Friend of mine at *Publishers' Journal.* He wants me to cover the Miami Book Fair."

"Then you'll want to interview his Highness Lord Ira."

"I'd rather he didn't know about my assignment," Luther said. "He'd want me to turn it into a puff story for Ripov Publishing."

"Aye, he would that."

"Have you seen him?"

"I think he's up in his office."

"With his assistant, Caroline?"

Bram shrugged. "Don't know. She's a nice piece of goods."

"I guess so, if you're shopping."

Bram smiled. "Ah, you're one of those faithful husbands. My book seems to attract young pretties who show up at book signings wanting to be bitten on the neck. They think I'm the vampire."

"Maybe you wear that cross to ward them off."

"At least it discourages the churchy ones."

"And the rest?"

"Not to tell, boyo. Not to tell."

Luther left Bram to his plinking on the piano and started back to his compartment to work on the article before dinner but took a wrong turn. Instead of the stairs down to the guests' quarters, he discovered another way down from the upper deck. Thinking it was an alternate route, he found himself at the owner's stateroom.

Curious, he tried the door. It wasn't locked and he opened it a bit to have a look. The cabin took the whole width of the Lollipop. In the center was a large, unmade double bed. He noticed women's underwear on the floor besides the bed and attached to each of the posts at the foot of the bed a pair of handcuffs. *So*, Luther thought. *A little S&M bondage. I wonder who's the sadist and who the masochist?* The owner's stateroom had its own private bath, and Luther heard the sound of water running.

He was about to shut the door when Ira Ripov's assistant Caroline came out of the bath. Was she the dominatrix to have her way with the handcuffed Ira Ripov? Or was she the one to submit to whatever might be done to her while handcuffed to the bed? That was something to think about.

Caroline was a dish, alright, with breasts fuller than Devra's. Luther felt an involuntary swelling in his loins. Caroline's tan revealed the white patches at her breasts that were normally covered by a very small bikini. She wore a ring in her pierced navel and below that her pubic hair had been shaved in the pattern called the "landing strip." What remained of her pubes were blonde, too. She saw Luther and continued to dry herself off, not taking any special care to cover herself up.

"Excuse me," Luther apologized. "I took a wrong turn."

She made no attempt to cover herself and seemed to enjoy his stare. "Seen enough?"

Luther was embarrassed, made a lame excuse. "Didn't come looking for anything."

As if an explanation were needed, she said, "Needed a shower. It's so muggy."

Her excuse was shattered when Ira Ripov came out of the bath in all his naked glory, saggy paunch and the breasts typical of older men. Perhaps he was taking hormones to combat a prostate problem. Ripov might be small in stature, but he was surprisingly well endowed, a penis like a salami.

Well, Luther thought. *That explains a lot of things*.

"Piss off, Luther," Ira said, angry. "These quarters are off limits." No "dear boy" this time.

"Sorry," Luther stammered. "Accident. Got lost."

"Well get lost and close that door behind you."

So Ira Ripov than an appetite for things other than money.

Luther closed the door and hurried back to his cabin.

Twelve

Luther got out his Apple laptop and opened the file. He was at a loss, now. There were too many angles to take on the story that didn't fit the outline he had sketched. He needed a central theme to tie it all together.

Maybe he should use the personality of Ira Ripov as the unifying theme. Ego had to be part of it, otherwise he wouldn't have used his own name for the name of his company. That wasn't unusual. Hadn't Henry Ford named his company after himself? Other owners had done the same, like Mr. Sears and his partner Roebuck, and Mr. Hershey.

It was not only an ego booster for people who liked to see their name in lights, but it was an attempt to transcend their own mortality. A corporation was an entity that could survive the death of its founder if it didn't go broke or was sold to someone else. But those companies' names didn't necessarily reflect their owner's or founder's personalities. You couldn't know what kind of a person Mr. J. C. Penney was by walking into his store.

Deciding to use an old yacht like the Lollipop as his headquarters and residence was unusual. An office building suite would have been more conventional, with the benefit of basement parking, security cameras and plumbing that worked. Big as the boat was, it didn't lend itself to expansion. From what Luther had seen, the yacht was hardly seaworthy. Those diesel engines didn't look like they'd been run in a long time, and the constant thumping of the bilge pump didn't bode well if the Lollipop were to ever leave the dock.

Did Ripov actually own the Lollipop? Or did he lease it? Maybe he had a big mortgage. If Ripov didn't pay his mooring fees, as the harbor master had claimed, and if he didn't pay his bar bill, either, or royalties for his authors, was it because Ripov was a cheap bastard or because his business was sinking? Maybe his acting the Billy Goat Gruff was an expression of his own desperation, trying to keep not only the Lollipop but his business afloat.

Luther hadn't thought of that before. He had thought only of his own royalties or lack of and of Ripov's insistence of tight control of everything, including purse strings.

Maybe Devra could provide him with some answers. He popped open his cell phone, saw that there was a good signal, even inside the yacht, and dialed.

She was at work in the blood lab at the VA hospital. "Hi, honey," she said.

"You got my message?"

"Only that you arrived in Miami without being hijacked by Arab terrorists. How's the Good Ship Lollipop?"

"Not such a good ship. If the bilge pumps quit I think she'll sink at the dock. Are you busy?"

"Kind of."

"There's no Wi-Fi here on the boat. Maybe you can Google Ira Ripov when you get home. Particularly the publishing company, not the web site. We've been through that and the history of the yacht, but there have to be more hits about the man himself. He pestered the authors about having blogs, Facebook, twitter and that stuff. He probably has some such sites himself."

"What are you looking for?"

"It's about my article for Charlie Broadbottom. Ripov's into some kinky stuff. He's a public figure. There must be stuff about him we can find out."

Devra was suspicious. "What sort of kinky stuff?"She had already made a remark about sex starved writers of erotica. Didn't she trust him?

"Besides S&M with his sexy assistant, he's got a crew of illegal immigrants who are practically slaves on the yacht and he owes money to everybody."

"I'll see what I can find out," Devra said.

"You don't have much time. The book fair is tomorrow and I'll be back early in the afternoon the day after. I've a reservation for an early morning flight."

She promised to so some web surfing. "I've got to go. Catch you later." She hung up.

It was stifling in the cabin. The heavy rains had only increased the Florida humidity. Luther unlatched the dogs holding the porthole shut and swung it open. The rain had let up. Maybe Greta really was heading out to sea. The little electric fan above the wardrobe hummed as usual, but didn't seem to move air more than a foot from the blades.

Luther studied his notes on the laptop, added a few comments. Charlie Broadbottom wouldn't want what he called a shotgun story, a smattering of facts without a unifying theme. Should he make the focus on Ripov Publishing a microcosm of the entire faltering publishing industry?

But Luther didn't know much about the industry. He'd lived in his own circumscribed world, eking out a living as an adjunct instructor with three crowded classes and a ton of papers all the while dreaming that his revised and revised and revised academic novel would somehow bring him enough riches for him and Devra to move into a bigger apartment.

Pipe dreams. He was little better off than Sally the barmaid who was maybe going to write a novel some day, or that deputy with his screen play. Some people did succeed. Stephen King had lived in a trailer and banged out short stories beside the water heater for years of apprenticeship until he finally made it big. But he worked at it, really worked at it, hammered out stories eight hours a day like some shift worker in a factory. And Rawlings, living on the dole, had kept warm in a café with her baby parked beside her while she scribbled Harry Potter on note pads.

They were exceptions. How many Kings and Rawlingses were there in the world? Half a dozen?

Hoping to be a hit author was worse than being the black kid who played basketball on an asphalt court in a school playground and dreamed of being an NBA star. The hopeless odds for that kid were better than his, and authors didn't get multi million dollar contracts for playing a game.

Luther wasn't tall enough for basketball, wasn't a good ball handler, and besides, he was white. Even black authors had a certain mystique, a certain novelty, being mainly out of the mainstream of the white New York publishing world.

And what about Ira Ripov? What were his prospects as a publisher in a depressed economy? Had he previously been an editor for a major that got gobbled up by a conglomerate? In years past being an editor at Random House meant virtually lifetime employment, but with the consolidation, seasoned editors found themselves out on the street as new management took over to dump the mid list authors and the editors who used to nurture them. With the accountants snapping at their heels like a pack of Dobermans, if their choices of books didn't sell, they were out.

The Miami book fair might well be a make or break event to determine the fate not only of Ira Ripov Publishing but of all the authors on his list.

The very thought exhausted Luther. It was easy to get depressed. Every time he went into Powell's bookstore he was confronted with thousands of titles all done by authors as hungry as himself, few with any real prospects. What a lousy business.

He shut down the laptop, set it on top of the bureau beside his shaving kit, turned his face toward the open porthole in the hopes of a breath of fresh air, and decided to sleep on it. Sometimes sleeping on a subject gave the unconscious mind a chance to ruminate and come up with answers. Luther hoped it would just be nightmares.

Thirteen

Luther was awakened by a gong and Jesus walking down the companionway calling "Dinner!" Groggy with the drugged-like sleep that sometimes comes in hot weather, he sat up on the edge of his bunk and shoved his feet into his loafers. They were still damp from his foray ashore with Mary S-- in search of spiders.

He felt something crunch as his right foot slipped into the shoe. Alarmed, he pulled his foot out to find he had crushed one of Franz K--'s dreaded Palmetto bugs. *Yuck! They must be everywhere. Maybe he should hunt up a couple of wolf spiders himself. At least they weren't rats.*

Ernest, wearing a pair of safari cargo shorts with big pockets, met him in the hallway. "I wonder what Maria has cooked up for us tonight? Want to get together at the Port o' Call after? We could round up the others and make a party of it."

"The Port O' Call would be neutral ground," Luther said. "If there's going to be a mutiny on this bounty it's best not to plan while on board."

At the foot of the stairs leading up to the main deck Luther tugged at Ernest's sleeve. "I stumbled onto Ripov's stateroom. Pretty posh quarters. Double bed complete with handcuffs. Guess who was coming out of the shower?"

"It wouldn't be Maria."

"Caroline. Buck naked. Ripov right behind. "

"I could tell she was hot. Handcuffs, you say? Must have been quite a party. Wonder if she goes for threesomes. Got to hand it to the old guy."

"Blame it on Viagra." Luther had read that with the advent of Viagra there was a huge increase of STDs among the senior citizens in south Florida.

Ernest had a second thought and shook his head. "What a woman has to endure to keep her job."

Luther added, "And what kind of a man takes advantage of her."

The authors assembled around the dining room table. Caroline sat next to Ripov and gave Luther a knowing look that said "You've seen me naked. There's more." Ripov gave Luther a disapproving scowl before welcoming his stable of authors. "Tomorrow's the big day, boys and girl. Unfortunately, there's no lunch on the book fair schedule, just time for shoppers to circulate, so we have to make sure our booth is ready for business. Our award ceremony is scheduled as part of the banquet that follows."

It promised to be a long, tiring day.

"I hope there's air conditioning," Franz K-- commented. This time he had ditched not only the waistcoat but the jacket as well and wore a gaudy Hawaiian shirt that was out of character for someone usually so conservative and withdrawn. Perhaps under that usually conservative demeanor there lurked a rebellious spirit.

"Just to get you all in the right mood," Ripov said, "I've brought up some vintage champagne. Did I tell you the original builder of the Lollipop installed a hidden wine cellar below the waterline?"

Jesus, wearing his white waiter's jacket, hefted a magnum bottle out of an ice bucket on the sideboard. Jesus seemed a bit mellow for a change. Perhaps he'd done some below the waterline sampling on his own. There was more to be done down there in the bilge besides check the pump. Jesus expertly popped the cork without spilling and filled everyone's champagne glass. There was just enough to go once around the table.

Ripov raised his glass. "To success."

Without much enthusiasm, the authors raised their glasses and drank. Some of Ripov's trickled into his beard.

Maria had prepared a dinner of chicken done Haitian style, or at least that's what Luther guessed must explain the unusual spices.

He wondered if the chickens had first been part of some animal sacrifice. Goats' heads had been found in the Miami waterway. Was it voodoo? He'd read in the Oregonian about certain religious practices that had prompted a lawsuit in Miami by the SPCA. The judge had thrown the case out, saying that religious animal sacrifices were no more cruel or barbaric than what happened in slaughter houses on a daily basis.

Ernest was thoughtful, not talkative during the meal. He took what to Luther looked like an enormous cartridge out of his pocket and played with it. He had showed Luther his elephant gun before, but Luther hadn't seen the ammunition for it. He knew nothing about firearms.

Luther asked to have a closer look. He handled the cartridge gingerly like it might simply explode. "Jesus! Thus this looks big enough for a cannon."

Ernest launched into a lecture on firearms. "Made in England by Holland and Holland. It's the .700 Nitro Express. That cartridge is almost four and a half inches long. The regular price is a hundred bucks apiece, but I got mine off the Internet for $50. Of course, you don't need many of them."

Herman saw the cartridge and looked envious. "You could probably kill a whale with that."

If a cartridge sold for a hundred bucks, how much was the rifle that fired them? "What does your rifle cost?"

"You don't want to know, Luther. You could pay sixty grand for a new one. I won mine in a poker game from a very unhappy English Lord in Kenya."

"I can see how he'd be unhappy."

"I told him it was a fair trade. He won my Land Rover the night before."

"Not much use for elephant guns in South Florida."

"You never know what you might run into. Call it my souvenir of a King high straight flush." After retrieving his expensive cartridge Ernest announced, "Luther and I are going up the road to the Port O' Call bar for drinks afterward. Anyone care to join us?"

Luther couldn't resist a dig. "It's not bad. Clean and well lighted."

"I'll take a pass," Ripov said to everyone's relief. "Got preparations for the fair tomorrow." He was probably avoiding a confrontation with Sally over the unpaid bill for booze.

"I'll buy the first round," Ernest said.

That cheered up the group.

They all sensed that Maria was overworked. Acting like family, they carried their dirty dishes to the galley for her. She seemed grateful for their moral support. Then the authors gathered on deck to leave together.

Darkness comes quickly at the Miami latitude. no lingering sunset and dusk as there was in Portland half way to the North Pole. Fortunately, the rain had quit. Miami had a reprieve from the threat of Greta.

The humidity was so thick Luther was already sweating.

They all marched in a body up the ramp and up Crab Cake Cove Road to the Port O' Call.

Fourteen

Back in Portland when Devra S-- returned from her job at the blood lab her feet hurt and she was depressed. She was used to dealing with the old World War II vets, because those who still survived in spite of old war wounds and post war infirmities tended to be, if not contented with their lives, at least reconciled to their conditions. The Vietnam war vets often suffered from the echoes of what had been called shell shock in World War I, battle fatigue in World War II, and now was universally recognized as post traumatic stress disorder, PTSD. What got to Devra were the new guys, young, strapping tough Marines with fresh wounds from Iraq and Afghanistan, not simply the limbs lost from IEDs planted beside the roads, but the head injuries. There was no prosthesis for a damaged brain. The lab routine was to confirm the identity of the patient, name and last four digits of their social security number. Some had trouble remembering. They were lost souls, many so battered that they would never recover.

The wages of war were generations of wounded, damaged men, and now more and more women, who paid the price for decisions made by politicians who risked no more than the loss of the next election. It was hard not to be affected by those patients, even though Devra's job was limited to the blood lab. She was not a surgical nurse standing by while physicians picked shrapnel out of battered bodies. The blood she worked with was drawn in tubes, not flowing from incisions.

The work would probably come when she finished her nurses' training at OHSU, Oregon Health Science University next door to the VA.

It didn't help that Luther was away in Florida having a fine time on that grand yacht. They had both studied the internet photos of the Lollipop. He was probably having a fine old junket with his fellow authors. She and Luther were always together. When he made those bookstore appearances on the Coast, she went along. Now Devra felt left out and abandoned.

She almost felt inclined to accept the offer of lunch from Larry Kohn, the handsome young resident doctor from OHSU. The medical school supplied the VA with specialists to supplement the regular staff of primary care physicians. All she knew about young doctor Kohn was that he was a urologist and that he was married. He was probably one of those med students whose wife was the breadwinner while he studied. She also knew that all too often once the guy got his degree he dumped the wife. She didn't want any part of that combination. Who knew where a casual offer of lunch might lead? At least for now she'd turned down his offer.

As Devra dropped her purse on the couch inside the door to their tiny apartment and took off her shoes she noticed the telephone answering machine was blinking. She thought it might be another call from Luther. It wasn't.

"This is Rick Sharp at *New Week* magazine. We're doing a story and would like to interview Luther S-- for background information. Please give me a call back, any time." He left a cell phone number.

What kind of a story was it? Something about the Lollipop award, the Miami Book Fair, or could it be for a review of Luther's book, *Tracking Tenure*? He could use some publicity.

Devra tried to call Luther to pass on the information, but all she could leave was a voice mail message and she knew he seldom checked for those. He must have switched off his cell. She also knew he was nervous about his cell phone battery running down. After he left for the airport and the Red Eye to Miami she'd discovered he forgot to pack the charger.

With the three hour time difference between Portland and Miami, it was already evening at Crab Cake Cove. If she were going to look up Ira Ripov on the internet and have something to report when Luther called her back, she'd have to get busy.

She did so with some reluctance, because she hadn't had much lunch, just coffee and a small pre-packaged salad out of the cooler in what passed for a café in the VA main building. She was hungry. Before Luther left for Florida they had picked up a roast chicken at Fred Meyer's and the remains, though cold in the fridge, beaconed.

She popped what remained of the roast chicken in the microwave, gave it two minutes on high, and carried the plate to her computer. She had a PC and Luther an Apple, but since she used PCs at the hospital she was more comfortable with her older machine. Eating with her fingers and conscious that she might get grease on the keyboard, she powered up to do the research Luther needed.

The Wikipedia didn't list Ira Ripov. Fortunately it wasn't a common name like Tom Smith, for if it were there would be hundreds of Tom Smiths out there. Fortunately there were only two Ira Ripovs, one of which was a lawyer in California, a dog lover whose golden retriever had its own web site. There were more than a thousand hits on Google for Ira Ripov the publisher. Because Ripov was also the name of his company most of the entries were connected to the books he published.

There were a few personal references, one of which was Ripov's Facebook account. Devra had to look for Luther's list of passwords and login names in order to access Facebook, but after a couple of false starts got in.

There was a picture of Ira Ripov, a strange looking man in a yachting cap and a beard like Santa Claus but without that kindly look and no red suit. Was he trying to look like a wise Dumbledore sage, or was he simply too lazy to shave or too cheap to buy a razor? Maybe he was hiding a receding chin. Was there hair under that nautical hat?

Ripov's written profile of himself was innocuous. The only oddity was that he was a bird watcher. He might turn up in a bird watcher's internet group, comparing notes on his life list and his search for a rare urban parrot.

The trouble with Google--and the advantage for snoops-- was that if your name turned up anywhere in the universe, the search engine could find it, even something otherwise lost in the morgues of defunct newspapers. If it had been microfilmed and digitized in some library, it could turn up. There was no balance between the essential sites and sheer overload. All entries had the same weight.

Aha! There was Ira Ripov in a story in *The Examiner* newspaper. While in college Ripov had been arrested for a fraternity hazing incident. He'd been one of several pledges sent out on a scavenger hunt the university authorities considered racist. The upshot of the scandal was the fraternity was banned from the college, its charter suspended.

How one could be haunted by long past indiscretions.

Another story reported that Ripov had been sued for plagiarism along with one of the authors he published. Settled out of court for an undisclosed sum.

He'd lost in small claims court over some unpaid bills, a case that wouldn't normally make the internet, except it had been reported in a newspaper. Once your name got into print, there you were. The search engines said "Gotcha!"

It added up to Ira Ripov with a history of litigation and acrimony. He was a man who made enemies.

There was even, remarkably, a picture of a young Ira Ripov, sans beard, in his high school yearbook from Scranton, Pennsylvania. Each picture on the page was accompanied by some little phrase like, "Most congenial" or "Future space engineer." In Ripov's case he was called "The Mean Machine."

In a group picture in the same yearbook Ira Ripov was pictured with the debating club, the smallest in stature of the bunch, a head shorter than most. So he was also argumentative.

Considering the difficulty Luther had had communicating with the man, and the details Devra had seen in that contract for the book, none of this information was particularly surprising or enlightening. Ira Ripov was a mean bastard who didn't pay his bills. He could probably have qualified in high school as the least liked, the kind of student who, bullied, went out and bought guns for a Columbine like massacre.

No wonder he was so hard to deal with. The Facebook history, sort of a brief resume, indicated that Ripov had once worked for Simon & Shyster, a New York publisher, now part of a conglomerate. Devra speculated that he'd been fired for being incompatible with everyone in the office.

She assembled clips of the sources into a single file. If Luther could connect somehow to a Wi-fi source she'd send the information as an email attachment.

Only then did she turn to that long distance call from Rick Sharp at *New Week*.

Fifteen

The Port O' Call already had a collection of regular drinkers at the bar. The Lollipop authors pushed two tables together at the back of the room so they could all sit together. Ernest, uncomfortable sitting for long periods because of his back injury, stood leaning against the window sill.

They had all joined him--Luther S--, Mary S--, Herman M--, Franz K--, even Bram S-- who declined alcohol, probably preferring to be sober in case he encountered a vampire. Ernest ordered a couple of pitchers of beer. He made good on his promise to buy the first round, paid cash. Bram ordered a diet Coke.

"You're the authors?" Sally said as she delivered the two pitchers of beer and the glasses on a tray. As a wannabe novelist, she obviously considered her customers to be celebrities, possibly as providers of collectible autographs.

Luther, reinforcing his memory of their names, introduced them. "This here is Ernest, big game hunter, Mary, monster expert, Franz our student of law, Herman the whale catcher, and non-alcoholic Bram, the vampire hunter. I'm just ordinary. I teach." Luther said. "Authors are just ordinary people, nothing to get too excited about."

"That's right," Ernest said. "We all put our pants on the same way, except, maybe Mary here."

Luther had to admit they were not ordinary at all. In fact, all they had in common was that they were authors. They didn't write in the same genre. If they were all mystery writers, that might have been a source for conversation. Or if they were writers of erotica they might compare notes on how to write sex scenes. The only other commonality was they were all on Ira Ripov's list, except, of course, their peculiar quirk of living in their pseudonyms. Luther didn't know any of their real names.

Herman didn't agree. "Authors have to have in common a desire to see their names in print. They also have to have unrealistic aspirations, dreams of fame and glory."

"But not like Rock Stars," Ernest added. "No groupies waiting outside the bookstore to snip a lock of your hair or tear your clothes off for souvenirs."

"Thanks to God for zat," Franz said. "If zat's what being a star author means, I'll keep my manuscripts in a drawer."

"That's no way to make a living," Sally said.

"The rule," Ernest advised, "is don't quit your day job. Luther here teaches at a university. Stick to bartending, Sally. Think of the tips."

"Which reminds me." She turned to serve another customer, a scruffy sport fisherman wearing a shirt that said "Anglers do it on the water."

As he filled his glass from the pitcher Ernest asked, "Any of you been to a book fair before?"

Franz had been to the one in Frankfort, Germany, but only as a spectator. "People come with shopping bags to load up on free copies," he said, lisping slightly.

"You think they read them?" Herman asked.

Franz shook his head. "I zink zey sell zem to used bookstores."

Ernest agreed. "That's what some reviewers do."

"I thought we were supposed to be signing and selling, not giving books away," Mary commented.

"If that's the case, how can Ripov expect us to sell anything?"

"Everybody wants something for nothing. Do we get any royalty on a book Ripov gives away, I mean, besides review copies?"

Franz wiped some foam off his upper lip. "Zat depends on the details in your contract."

"We're not supposed to disclose the details of our contracts," Herman said, and looked around in case someone might be eavesdropping.

The others in the Port O' Call appeared to be sports fishermen confined to the port because of the bad weather. It was just as well that Ripov and Caroline hadn't joined them.

Ernest shifted his weight uncomfortably. Standing at the window gave him a physical presence of authority, even though it was because of his back that he was standing, not because he wanted to be the leader. "If we're having a council of war, I think we can blow off Ripov's non disclosure agreement."

They compared notes. Without having the actual texts at hand, it appeared that Ripov used a canned, stock contract written up by a lawyer determined to lock up all rights and leave the author no wiggle room or opt out options. Not only that, but Ripov got first refusal on prequals and sequels.

"It could be worse," Franz commented. "Some publishers not only vant to own the rights to your books, but to own ze characters. If a book establishes a character worthy of a series, such as Sherlock Holmes, James Bond or Trixie Belden, some publishers vant ownership of the character. Zen zey have ze option of continuing ze series using other writers. Zey can even shut out the original author completely. Zis might be OK in case ze original author dies, but if Ripov wanted to, and zat vas in our contracts, he could go on with a series and cease printing ze author's own work, sitting on all rights and leaving ze author with nothing. Vat do you zink of zat?"

This, they all agreed, was intolerable.

Bram did not want anyone else using his vampire.

Herman laid full claim on rights to his whale.

Mary did not approve of people copying her monster.

Luther did not think anyone would be interested in the further misadventures of the hapless tenure seeking instructor in his book, but he agreed with the others.

Though nothing anyone could remember of their contract with Ripov gave him the right to derivative works using their copyrighted characters, there was no opt out clause. If Ripov's numerous creditors forced him into bankruptcy and his list were sold, the buyer was not obligated to publish anything or release any rights back to the original authors.

They were all stuck, unless someone could figure out a way out of it. "How do you know all this?" Luther asked Franz. He was feeling like a babe in the woods.

"I studied law in Europe," Franz explained. "Surely you read your contracts before you sign zem."

Luther was ashamed to admit that he was so eager to see his book published, to get an acceptance after all, that he was glad enough to sign a contract with any terms. The business of prequels and sequels didn't strike him as relevant. Wasn't it like signing a lease on their apartment in Portland stipulating no pets? Since they had no pets, so what? He had no plans for other books about his struggling professor. But he had heard that readers liked series, became familiar with the characters, and wanted to read more about them. Series books, like the Sylvia Plum mysteries, sold well.

"So what happens tomorrow?" Herman asked no one in particular.

Franz had a suggestion. "Ira Ripov has first refusal on our next books, right? But if he doesn't pay ze royalties as stipulated in ze contract, he is in default. Ze contract is void."

That sounded plausible to Luther, but what about that business of binding arbitration? Could be a battle.

Franz wasn't finished. "There will be many other publishers at ze fair. Besides selling our books, I zink we should shop around. Make contacts. If Ripov goes broke, we will need new publishers."

One thing the contracts could not demand was loyalty. Loyalty could not be bought. It had to be earned, and Ira Ripov was not the sort of man who inspired loyalty. If anything he alienated people. He might flatter on occasion or tell a good joke, turn on the charm, but it was a thin veneer.

The conversation turned to other matters. Luther revealed his chance encounter with the nude Caroline and made a discreet reference to Ripov's prodigious male organ.

Mary S-- was interested. "And you say there were handcuffs on the bed posts? Ira Ripov, you naughty man!" She almost blushed. It sounded like she might give Ripov a try herself.

Luther sensed Mary's availability. What sort of sex life did she have since her husband drowned? He could see that book fair junkets were an opportunity for hanky panky away from home. He also knew that one such misstep could ruin a marriage and a career. Too many politicians had destroyed themselves with such liaisons.

His beer glass was almost empty. So was the second pitcher the bar maid Sally had brought. He refilled his glass and, feeling flushed with the beer and a desire to be a good sport, ordered another pitcher. When it came he realized that he'd better pay with his Visa card in case he had unexpected demands on his limited cash. He never used ATM machines and even if he needed one, couldn't remember his PIN.

Thinking about another night aboard the bug-infested Lollipop, he turned to Franz. "Can I borrow one of your wolf spiders? I found one of your pet palmetto bugs in my shoe."

Herman wanted to know about wolf spiders and Mary S-- launched into an entomological discussion. Nature was her passion, whether it was lighting bolts or bugs.

Outside the Port O' Call there was a distant rumble of thunder. More rain was in the offing and none of them had worn raincoats or brought an umbrella. It was already late, so they retired to the Lollipop, arriving at the dock just in time for the first splatters of another heavy rain.

In his absence Maria had made the bed in his cabin and laid out fresh towels. Besides being cook she had to work hard for whatever wages Ripov paid if she were paid at all.

Would she be tempted to steal? Luther made sure his laptop was still in the drawer. It was, along with his return ticket to Portland. Nothing was missing.

Luther was slow in getting ready for bed and had to wait his turn with his toothbrush and towel in the companionway outside the only functioning guest bathroom. The door to the crew's quarters and the engine room access was open, probably for some air circulation. If his cabin was small, how much more pristine were the quarters for Jesus and Maria? In its grand old days, how big a crew did the Lollipop require? Captain and first mate and what? Four more? From down below he heard the steady rumble of the bilge pump.

What time was it back in Portland? He'd better call Devra.

Sixteen

Devra answered on the first ring. "I was hoping you'd call. I got a file of stuff on Ira Ripov. And there was a call from Rick Sharp at *New Week* magazine. He wants you to call him back."

"What about?"

"Didn't say. Might be an interview about your book."

"I can't believe that." If the lack of royalty checks was any indicator, his book was a flop, not even a ripple in the sea of over three hundred thousand books being published that year in the United States alone.

"Call him and find out." Devra gave him the number.

He wrote it down. "Okay. What did you find out about Ripov?"

"He's been in and out of trouble. College mischief. Sued for plagiarism. Taken to small claims court. All small stuff."

"At least he's not a criminal," Luther said. "It wouldn't be very lucrative. Stealing from authors is hardly a way to make money."

Devra was not so sure. "He seems to attract trouble and make enemies. There are bastards and there are dirty, rotten bastards."

"He's a dirty old man and he may be rotten, but I don't know about his parentage." He told her about his chance encounter in the owner's stateroom. He didn't go into the details of Caroline's shaved pudendum.

"You'd better watch yourself," Devra cautioned.

Luther was reminded of that funny movie about the woman in the red dress in which the lustful wannabe philanderer ends up standing on a ledge outside a hotel room window wearing only a woman's robe and despairing that he got into all that trouble just for a piece of ass. "Not worth it."

"As for Ripov, if you can get on the internet read your email. I've sent you the file as an attachment."

"I'll take my laptop to the fair in the morning. They should have Wi-fi there."

"And don't forget to call that guy at *New Week*."

"Will do."

"How's the weather?"

"It's raining." When conversations drifted into the weather, people had run out of important things to say. What difference did it make to Devra if it was raining in Miami? It was probably raining in Portland. It usually was.

"The weather report said something about a hurricane."

"Greta went out to sea. But if I fly to Florida again I'll bring some waterproof pants. My cycling jacket just covers my butt."

She rang off with a parting "Love you."

Luther poked the numbers of Rick Sharp at *New Week* magazine.

It rang three times before the party picked up.

"This is Luther S-- in Miami. You talked to my wife, said you wanted to contact me."

"Yes. I just wanted some information on Ira Ripov."

"What sort of information?" Luther didn't know the real purpose of the call. If *New Week* were doing a story, he didn't want to kill his own article.

"There's some suspicion that Ira Ripov Publishing isn't entirely legitimate."

"Just because Ripov doesn't pay his bills doesn't mean he's illegitimate. He's just tight, or maybe a poor bookkeeper."

Rick Sharp had other ideas. "He's got that yacht, doesn't he?"

"Yes, and his crew are a couple of illegal immigrants, but that's nothing special."

"You think he uses that yacht-- what's it called?"

"Lollipop. It's the good ship Lollipop."

"Lollipop," Sharp corrected. "Could he use the Lollipop to smuggle in illegal immigrants?"

Luther had to laugh. "Not bloody likely. If this derelict weren't tied to the dock I think it would sink."

Sharp was groping. "There are rumors that the publishing business is just a front. Could Ripov have been laundering money for Barny Madoff, the ponzi swindler?"

Luther couldn't believe that. "If Ira were laundering money he'd be skimming a bunch for himself and living fat." Skimming from some criminal activity was a sure way of finding yourself full of bullets in the trunk of a stolen car abandoned in an airport long term parking lot. Madoff didn't look like the Mafia type, just your friendly, scheming, con artist with no conscience "I think Ira Ripov is just someone people would like to pin something on. Whoever gave you that tip is just fishing. Who is it? The IRS?"

"Can't say."

Did Sharp mean he would not reveal his source or that he didn't know? "Well, I don't think I can help you, Mr. Sharp." Clearly Sharp wasn't giving any details and Luther didn't want to give away the fact that he was under an assignment from a competing publication.

Sharp wasn't giving up. "You'll be at the Miami Book Fair tomorrow?"

"That's the plan. We're piling into an old station wagon at eight o'clock in the morning. Ripov is going to hand out the first annual Lollipop Award, whatever that is."

"You may be contacted by someone from *New Week* at the fair."

"Maybe they'll buy my book," Luther said, remembering to never miss a chance to plug his product. "*Tracking Tenure.* It's an academic novel."

"I'm through with academia," Sharp said. "I was glad to get out of grad school with my hide intact. Talk about exploitation!"

Could life at *New Week* be any better? Every profession had its politics, whether it was in a classroom or like Dolly Parten, working nine to five in her movie of the same name. In that one the exploited women gang up on the lecherous boss. The tune rattled in his head. What about exploited authors ganging up on their stingy publisher? That was a thought. You didn't have to be at sea to stage a mutiny.

"If that's all, I've got to get some sleep. Good night, Mr. Sharp." Luther turned off his cell phone. What the hell did *New Week* want from him, anyway? Luther was hardly an insider, and he wasn't going to gossip to *New Week* about Ira Ripov's sexual adventures with his assistant. He wasn't writing for the *Enquirer* or one of the scandal mongering grocery store magazines. No photos of Caroline, like some Paris Hilton debutante "going commando" and caught getting out of a car with her legs apart. That was not his kind of story.

The tiny cabin was stuffy, the humidity so high putting on a shirt meant instant sweat. The little fan over the bureau smelled like the motor was overheated. Luther opened the porthole but that let in the rain again. He reluctantly closed it and dogged down the latches. It wasn't entirely tight. The aged bronze porthole frame had warped over the years. The original gasket was long gone and a trickle of water seeped in and ran down the varnished wall, threatening to soak the bed.

Luther took down the hand towel he had carried to the bathroom and wiped the wetness away. If he couldn't keep dry, it was going to be a long, uncomfortable night. He would sleep on top of the sheets, no blanket, if he could sleep at all. Were there more of those damned Palmetto bugs? He must remember to shake his shoes out before he put them on in the morning.

Seventeen

Luther woke to the gentle but ominous movement of the Lollipop. He had slept badly, stifled by the Florida heat and humidity. The little electric fan over the bureau had smelled overheated the night before. Now it had stopped. He flicked the switch a couple of times. Nothing. The lamp still worked, so there was electric power. If Ira Ripov wanted to retain the antique authenticity of the Lollipop he would be hard pressed to find a replacement fan that matched the period. Maintaining a yacht must be very expensive. Maintaining an old museum piece like the Lollipop must cost a fortune.

He wiped the condensation off the porthole and looked out to see an almost deserted cove disturbed by swells that hooked around the mole at the entrance. Somewhere offshore Greta was still hovering, sending out a menacing harmonic of heavy seas. It was raining heavier than ever.

He suspiciously shook his loafers and looked inside to make sure he hadn't picked up a resident cockroach. He was trying to remember what he was going to wear for the book fair when he heard Jesus ringing a gong in the companionway. "Breakfast!"

It was barely seven o'clock. Ira Ripov had warned them that at eight they'd be riding in the fake woodie wagon to downtown Miami.

Mary S-- had already occupied the single bathroom, leaving Bram with his cross and garlic necklace--he must sleep with that stuff-- and Franz, unkempt and unhappy in striped pajama bottoms that resembled concentration camp uniforms, both waiting impatiently in the companionway outside the bathroom door. Luther decided he could shave later and started for the stairs, nearly losing his balance as the Lollipop lurched and ground against her fenders. No wonder some people got seasick without even leaving the dock.

Up in the dining room, Herman was enjoying the rough weather. His eyes glistened with excitement behind his thick eyeglasses. "Morning, Luther!" He waved a fork in the direction of the rain-drenched windows. "No need to go to sea. It's come to us."

Maria, unsteadily carrying a tray from the galley, looked pale. Luther knew only a few words of French, said "Bon jour," and received only a nod and a wan smile in response. "Seasick?"

She didn't understand.

"She's not a good sailor," Herman said as if the cook and maid needed an interpreter.

Luther loaded a plate with scrambled eggs, bacon, and Win-Dixie white toast. The weak coffee tasted like the water had been poured through yesterday's grounds. "So today's the big day. Going to bring your harpoon to the fair?"

"Don't leave home without it," Herman said with a wink. "What's your trade mark?"

"I guess I don't have one. My laptop, I suppose."

"What are you writing now? Another book?"

"I thought I'd write about the book fair. Free lance. See if the Oregonian will take something."

Herman gave him a knowing look. "You should try one of the tabloids. Sneak a photo of Caroline and Ripov together. Headline: publisher caught in sex scandal."

"Ira Ripov's not important enough for that. Nowadays for a sex scandal you have to be at least a governor or a major celebrity."

"But you have taken pictures."

Luther had his digital in his pocket. "Unfortunately, the best shots happen when you're not ready for them."

"At least with a tiny camera like that you aren't obtrusive, not like the old days when photographers lugged around a speed graphic with a big flash attachment and bulbs that sometimes exploded."

"Before my time," Luther admitted. He couldn't remember when he last used film. But it was a good reminder, and he stood up, got Herman to pose for a photo, than caught the others as they came into the dining room. They were not well composed shots, but they could be cropped later.

Ira Ripov joined them at table. He not only had his ever present yachting captain's cap with the gold braid but had donned a blazer with an anchor applique on the pocket. His copious beard had been brushed into a shining, white mane, and he looked full of himself.

Luther got his picture, too.

"Well boys and girl, are we ready for the big show? My assistant Caroline's gone on ahead to set up our booth and I've drawn up a schedule, two hours on for each of you in the morning, same in the afternoon, but there have to be three at lunch hour when there's the most traffic. You mustn't be naughty and sneak off before the award's ceremony at the banquet. We need to make a big splash."

As if to emphasize his point, a wave crashed against the hull of the Lollipop as a freak wave rolled over the breakwater and swept along the hull. The Lollipop shuddered like a sleeping dog awakened by a bad dream. Something fell in the galley, the sound of breaking crockery.

The table of authors looked nervously at each other.

"Don't worry, boys and girl," Ripov said not very convincingly. "We are perfectly safe here. Crab Cake Cove is what they call a hurricane hole." He looked at his watch. "Get your paraphernalia together. Ernest, I assume you're taking along your elephant shooter."

Ernest nodded. He was dressed for safari. "Like Herman here says, don't leave home without it."

Luther asked, "Will we be back in time for me to get some sleep before an early morning flight back to Oregon?"

"Surely you're not in a hurry to leave this congenial company, dear boy."

It was hard for Luther to decide whether Ripov was sincere or being ironic. "If our work here is done..." He let the sentence trail off.

Ripov gave him a patronizing smile reserved for small children who knew nothing. "In this weather I suspect all flights will be canceled. You may be my guest for longer than you think."

Luther resolved to pack his things before leaving for the fair in case it were possible for him to make a quick getaway. He'd take his laptop to the book fair and check on reservations on line. There was certain to be a Wi-fi service at the convention hotel.

He'd be able to recharge the Apple's depleted battery at the same time. It had been fully charged before he left Portland but laptop batteries never performed as advertised. He'd been disappointed that there was no 110 volt service in his cabin. Ripov had a computer in his office behind the bridge, but apparently only part of the Lollipop was wired for that shore power. What was the rest of the yacht running on?

Thirty-two volts? Must be an inverter someplace. That generator down in the engine room didn't run all the time, only when the shore power was out.

He wished his internet sources had provided a more complete history of the yacht. There were no technical specifications other than the yacht's length and girth and a brief reference to diesel engines being replaced for service during the war. The next owner, the dot com millionaire, had attempted a restoration that apparently wasn't complete when the bubble burst.

Being in Florida was a bit of an adventure, but being basically confined to the Lollipop and headed for the Miami Book Fair he was hardly a tourist. That bathing suit and sunscreen he had packed were wishful thinking. There had never been a moment for lounging on the deck and he had no need for the sunscreen Homeland Security had confiscated.

Luther would be glad to get home where he didn't have to check his shoes in the morning for hitchhiking Palmetto bugs. Portland was infamous for its winter rains, but it was never as humid and stifling as buggy and muggy Florida.

Luther excused himself, went down to his cabin, had that delayed shave, and packed for a quick escape.

Eighteen

Jesus had the fake woodie wagon ready at the head of the dock. The swells rolling off Biscayne Bay made the floating sections rock like the unsteady floor of a fun house. The troupe of Lollipop authors straggled up the slippery ramp in the rain. Luther wore his yellow cycling jacket, Mary S-- in her blue raincoat clutched her umbrella. Bram, his collar turned up, wore a shabby raincoat and a floppy, shapeless hat. Herman M--, looking like some fisherman off the grand banks, had somehow produced a genuine so'wester seaman's hat and slicker. He carried his harpoon at the ready like some shore-bound Captain Ahab. Ernest toughed it out, sans rain gear, but carrying his gun case.

Ira Ripov met them at the car. He was wearing a tough, Heli Hansen commercial fisherman's yellow foul weather jacket, but not the bib pants or boots.

It was a full load. Jesus drove, Mary in the middle of the front seat, Ira Ripov alongside. Poor, grumbling Franz was squeezed way in the back with Bram, like a couple of kids on their way to a Little League game. Luther was stuck in the middle of the back seat between a harpoon and an elephant gun. He persuaded Herman to hold the harpoon, point down, against the door. If they hit a bump he didn't want to be speared. He also hoped that the elephant gun Ernest hugged between his knees in its case wasn't loaded. If they hit a bump and that cannon went off it would blow a huge hole in the roof of the car taking Ernest's head with it.

The windshield wipers flapping at full speed but with little effect, the wagon splashed through the nearly flooded Crab Cake Cove road, lurching through the potholes and out to the highway and on toward downtown Miami.

Luther was glad he wasn't driving, for it was like driving through a car wash. The highway looked like a river. What if Jesus took a wrong turn and drove into a canal?

The entrance to the convention hotel was fortunately under a marquis. The group decompressed out of the station wagon. Ira Ripov got out first and handed each of his stable of authors their ID pouches which they dutifully hung around their necks.

"Your banquet tickets are inside," Ripov explained. "We have a table reserved so you'll all sit together for the awards ceremony."

Ah, yes. The Lollipop award. Luther had nearly forgotten.

Before going inside the hotel Mary S-- stood watching the rain. "Isn't it wonderful?"

"It rains in Oregon," Luther said, "But nothing like this. Portland's rain is usually gentle and it doesn't rain all the time. Even when it does it's usually a gentle soak that turns the hills into chocolate pudding that slides down onto the streets taking houses with it. This is more like, well, India."

"The monsoon," Mary said. "Nature! Don't you love the lightning?"

"Not particularly."

"It energizes me. Makes me want to cavort naked in the rain." She gave him a wink.

Now that was a thought. Luther was imagining Mary dancing nude in the rain when a crash of thunder sent him scurrying indoors.

The convention hall was a cacophony of noise and activity. All the major publishers were there, taking up the largest displays and divided into sections for the various imprints. Pearson, the English holding company that owned Penguin and other imprints, vied for space with the five New York conglomerates. Smaller, independent publishers like Lollipop, were relegated to a second tier.

There was also a special section for the newcomers to publishing, the producers of electronic books. Amazon.com had a display of its Kindle ebook readers. The competitors offering other readers were in the same row. The battle for electronic book dominance had been joined. Sony, Apple, and a couple of others were vying for the attention of people willing to read books on the screens of their cell phones, iPods, blackberries, and other electronic gadgets.

In spite of that technology there were booths for traditional bookbinders who clung to the old ways and proudly displayed samples of their ornate craft, fragrant goatskin leather and gilded embossing.

Luther, who could claim only one debut novel to his name, felt out classed and utterly inadequate. It made him wonder why on earth Ira Ripov had ever added him to the list.

It was so unlikely that it made him believe there was something to Sharp's allegation that Lollipop Publishing was a front for something else like some Mafia restaurant that wasn't meant to make a profit. *New Week* magazine must have some information beyond Luther's imagination. Did Charlie Broadbottom have some inkling about that?

As soon as Luther had his Apple power supply plugged into a handy socket under the Lollipop display table, he excused himself and got out his cell phone. Inside the building he could get no signal.

He slipped outside to the entrance of the hotel, and stood under the canopy watching the rain sluice down like fire hoses beyond the shelter. Here, at least, if he could hear the phone over the noise of the rain hammering down, he could give Broadbottom a call.

Charlie Broadbottom answered on the second ring.

"Hi, Charlie. It's Luther. I'm at the Book Fair. Say, I got a call from a guy at *New Week* magazine. Wanted information about Ira Ripov. Suggested something shady. You know anything about that?"

"No. How are you coming on your piece?"

"I think the theme will be how a small publisher can survive in a sea of powerhouse competitors."

Broadbottom had another idea. "Sometimes while the big stags are fighting it out, the little guy sneaks in and mates with the does. The hope is that a sleeper book takes off and is then taken over by a major publisher. Look what happened to Rawlings. Her Harry Potter book got a test drive by a small publisher and when it was successful the majors stepped in."

"So *Tracking Tenure* has a chance?"

Broadbottom laughed, not unkindly. "In your dreams, Luther. In your dreams."

"So you don't know what *New Week* might be investigating?"

"Not a clue, but I'll ask around."

"If you do learn something, send me an email. There's Wi-fi here at the hotel but my phone won't work inside."

"Fair enough."

Email. Of course. Devra had told him she was sending a file on Ripov. Maybe there was something in that. Now all he had to do was access it without Ira Ripov snooping.

Nineteen

Caroline had set up a nice display of books by Lollipop authors. Ernest's, Bram's, Mary's, Herman's, and Franz's books all lent themselves to garish, dramatic covers. By comparison, Luther's *Tracking Tenure* looked dull. There was nothing in the design that, on display in a bookstore rack, would reach out and grab a browser saying "buy me." Instead, his cover told him "loser."

Caroline arranged a supply of brochures and catalogs. She also set out a bowl of Hershey's kisses to lure browsers to the display. She was dressed in the same red power suit open at the neck. He suspected there was no bra under it. Luther couldn't help staring, for he had seen the rest of her and remembered. It was certainly tempting.

She noticed his roving eye and winked. Was it an invitation?

Feeling guilty, he said, "Got to check my email." He opened his Apple laptop, powered up, and connected to the hotel Wi-fi signal. He logged on to his email account and amidst the spam and junk found the message from Devra.

The attachment she had assembled of information about Ira Ripov included the reference to the college incident, the picture of the debating team, the stories about the law suits. All shed a bit more light on Ira Ripov. That he had once worked for a major publisher, Simon and Shyster, showed that he had background in the publishing business but he hadn't stayed there long.

The debating team explained something about Ripov's iron fisted contracts. He'd encircle and demolish someone in an argument. His way of demeaning people with his "boys and girl" and "dear boy" was just a tactic to belittle and defeat.

"Something interesting?" Caroline asked, leaning over his shoulder so her bosom brushed his cheek. It was a deliberate tease.

Her intimacy made him nervous and he shifted away. He closed the laptop. Had she seen what he was reading? "Email from my wife. Private stuff."

She hadn't missed his retreat. "A faithful husband," she said. "A rarity." It was also a challenge.

Leaning over his shoulder, she'd braced her left hand on the table and he noticed a bruise on her wrist that might have been caused by the handcuffs he'd seen on Ripov's bedpost. "Hurt yourself?"

She had her other arm around his shoulder and he saw her right wrist had a bruise, too. "I think you know."

"He plays rough, doesn't he? How long have you worked for Mr. Ripov?"

"Too long. He hired me after he moved aboard the Lollipop."

"Are handcuffs part of the job description?"

"Jobs as executive assistant are hard to come by," she admitted.

Suddenly he felt sorry for her. How much did a woman have to be humiliated to get a job?

"My wife tells me he used to work at Simon and Shyster. Know anything about that?"

She didn't.

"He must have made a ton of money in New York to be able to afford that old yacht."

"If he did, it's about gone. This book fair has to save his bacon. If we don't get some orders I'll be looking for another job."

"Maybe something that doesn't demand hanky panky on the side?"

She didn't say. Luther remembered Ripov's debts, the unpaid marina fees, the bar bill at the Port O' Call. "And I'll be looking for another publisher," Luther said.

"This is the make or break deal," Caroline said. "Sell some books. And don't just concentrate on your own. When you're in this booth you're working for Ira Ripov Publishing, not just Luther S--."

"I get it."

Mary S-- came to the booth with a tray loaded with cups of coffee and donuts. "There's a table of refreshments for people who graze the displays and eat their breakfast standing up."

"Thanks." Luther picked a jelly donut and was immediately glad Mary S-- had remembered to include napkins. He didn't want sticky goop on his Apple keyboard.

A skinny kid with acne and a protruding Adam's apple neck came up to their display, took a couple of chocolates from the bowl. He had the eager look of an excited high school student or maybe a college freshman.

"Hi," Luther said. "Welcome to Ripov Publishing."

"You one of the authors?"

"Yes. I'm Luther S--. This is my book here."

"Hmm. *Tracking Tenure*. Sounds boring."

"It's about cutthroat academic politics with a love interest."

"Any sex?"

Luther admitted, "Not much."

"I write science fiction," the kid said, and produced his business card: Peter Piper, Author. It looked like he'd done it up himself on his home computer.

My god, another wannabe author, Luther thought. "Is your work published?"

"Yeh. I got two books out, science fantasy really."

"Who's your publisher?"

"I am," the kid said proudly. "I use Lulu.com for print on demand books. It's cool. Lulu connects them with Amazon, so you can find my books on the internet."

He hasn't a hope, Luther thought. "Any sales?"

Peter Piper grinned sheepishly. "Not on the best seller list yet. Sold five hundred copies so far."

"Really?"

"Yep. I set the price and there's no middle man. None of that 55% discount for distributors shit. There's the printing cost and I keep the difference. About thirty percent."

"Lulu, you say?"

"Yep."

"Maybe I'll try them for my next book," Luther said.

So far he hadn't seen even one percent of royalty from Ira Ripov. But next book? The contract with Ripov gave him first refusal on the next book. He was trapped by that dwarfish, bearded, cheapskate while that pimply kid was cleaning up in the book business as an independent. What the hell.

"There's the ebooks, too," Peter Piper said. "Your book electronic?"

"No."

"That's the wave of the future. People reading novels on cell phones."

"I couldn't imagine reading a book on a cell phone screen." It made Luther feel distinctly old fashioned. If that's where publishing was going, Ira Ripov and his stable of authors was sunk.

"Thanks for the candy," the kid said. "Good luck." He disappeared in the crowd.

Ira Ripov had been watching the exchange from a distance. Still wearing that captain's cap, he approached the booth. "Any customers?"

"Nothing yet," Luther admitted. "This is tough."

"It's a dog eat dog world, dear boy. You have to have sharp teeth in this business."

There's nothing quite as lonely as sitting at a booth at a fair when all any bored browser is interested in is the free chocolate on the bowl you've set out. They drift up, give your wares a cursory glance, and drift away without a word. Your product, the result of years of work, is on display and they aren't interested.

Luther was glad when it was Ernest's turn in the barrel. But Ernest, in his safari outfit and elephant gun attracted interest. People saw that double barreled firearm conversation piece and were instantly engaged.

Just before noon someone paid particular attention to Luther's name tag. "Luther S--?"

"That's what it says on the tag," Luther said, feeling cynical.

"You got a call from Rick Sharp, I believe."

"You're from, *New Week*?"

"Right. Rick told me I should find you here. Can we talk?"

Twenty

Luther excused himself, leaving Ernest in charge.

The man from *New Week* was in his forties, dressed in a dark suit, white shirt, tie. He was clean shaven. The sideburns of his otherwise dark hair had a distinguished gray. His eyes always seemed to be looking somewhere else, watchful. Only his first name, Arthur, was on the card inserted in the book fair ID pouch hanging around his neck.

Luther had the awkward sense that the man was a cop or maybe a detective. "We can talk in the lobby."

Though there were several people lined up at the registration desk, the soft chairs arranged around low tables were deserted. On the table where they sat Luther noticed a disheveled complimentary copy of the *Miami Herald*. The main front page story was about the hurricane. He hadn't heard a news broadcast or read a newspaper since he left Portland and was curious, but resisted the impulse to pick it up.

"What's up?"

"You're one of the Ripov Publishing authors."

"Right."

"And staying aboard the Lollipop?"

"Yes."

"Not in the hotel?"

"I think Mr. Ripov wants us to be together like a happy family. Or maybe so he can keep an eye on us. He's a controlling sort of a guy."

"Good observation," Arthur of no last name said.

"Or it could be that he's too cheap to lay out money for rooms at the convention hotel when he has a big old yacht with lots of guest cabins."

"That makes sense. What's your assessment of Ira Ripov?"

Luther thought about it. "He thinks he's cute, with that silly captain's cap and beard, but he isn't."

"Maybe we all wear masks," Arthur said.

"I'm not wearing a mask." Heck, he even used his own name. The others had donned pseudonyms like costumes. "Why did you pick me to interview? Did you call the others? They're far more interesting than I am."

Arthur smiled. "You're the only one with a phone number."

"What?"

"The other authors aren't in phone books. Their web sites don't have contact numbers. Maybe it's because once you're well known everyone pesters you."

"I'm unknown. I don't even have a web site," Luther admitted. He was working on it, but intimidated by the cost. He didn't want to admit that he didn't have the skills to set one up or the money to have a professional do it for him.

Arthur continued. "Ernest H-- isn't really Ernest H-- but someone else. The whole bunch of them--Franz K--, Mary S-- and so on. You're the only one willing to use your own name. The author info page at the back of your book says you live in Portland, so that's how we found you."

"They're eccentric. It's like a costume party."

"Right. But not you."

"Not me. I'm not putting on a front. What you see, is what you get."

"So you'll give me real answers, not something scripted."

Luther shrugged. "Why not?"

"So tell me about Ira Ripov."

"He's cheap. None of us has received a penny in royalties."

"Uh. Huh."

"The harbor master is ready to put a lien on the yacht because Ripov's mooring fees are in arrears."

Arthur nodded. The Miami Book Fair kit had come with a little plastic folder with pad and ballpoint. He took notes.

"I'm pretty sure his crew of two, a Cuban and Haitian are both undocumented."

"Interesting."

"He's also into S&M with his sexy assistant, Caroline."

"Cute."

"She says he started out with a chunk of money but now its all gone." Now Luther took a turn at a question. "Ripov used to work at Simon and Shyster, but left. What's the story behind that?"

"I was getting to that," Arthur explained. "Rumor in the trade has it that while Ripov worked at Simon and Shyster, S&S, he discovered they were fiddling the books."

"How's that?"

"You probably know that the major book distributors are notorious for being slow payers. They not only wait for the returns to come in, but if a publisher supplies, say, two hundred copies of a book and they are sent out to bookstores, then returned, the distributor may ask for credit for maybe two hundred and fifty. In the confusion of many orders to many stores, the publisher gets stuck for books never sent out."

"But that's the publisher's problem," Luther said. "What's that got to do with Ripov?"

"He found out that S&S made up for those losses by faking the sales orders and skimming from the royalty payments to the authors. In some cases that was for thousands of copies. Authors were getting ripped off."

"I know the feeling well," Luther said and wondered if the kid who used the on line printer lulu.com were getting cheated. If so, how could he tell?

Some printers were unscrupulous. If you ordered a batch of something, a poster, for instance, some would run a few hundred extra copies and sell them themselves. Since they prepared the offset plates and ran them on their machine, they kept possession of the plates. Only ethics prevented them from making copies for their own use. There was a difference between having copies as samples to show other customers the quality of their work and selling them.

There were crooks everywhere. The worst department store thieves weren't the shoplifters who stole a single item, but the employees who took stuff out the back door by the case. Then the honest customers paid for all the shrinkage in the form of marked up prices. You could easily conclude that everyone was dishonest.

Luther had subscribed to Googlealert. If his name or his book showed up anywhere on Earth, he'd be notified. He'd seen a used copy of *Tracking Tenure* for sale in a Bombay bookstore. How had a copy of his book made it to India? And where was his royalty for the original sale?

"So Ira Ripov threatened to blow the whistle on S&S. Expose the publisher by notifying all the authors of how much they'd been cheated."

"Unless what?"

"Unless they paid him to keep his mouth shut."

"Extortion," Luther said.

Arthur nodded. "They agreed to pay up if he never set foot in the place again."

"I get it. Sort of a golden parachute. So they got rid of him."

"But it backfired. You familiar with the trade? What goes on in New York publishing?"

"Not hardly. I'm on the West Coat in Portland, Oregon."

Arthur took a breath. "The irony is that the management at S&S thought they'd got rid of Ripov, but then the company was bought by Liechtenstein, a foreign conglomerate. Their accountants discovered the payments to Ripov, put a stop to them, and cleaned house. Fired the ones who paid off Ripov in the first place."

"Justice served," Luther said. "What goes around comes around."

"Sort of, but that doesn't close the books. There's still extortion and fraud."

"So is anyone going to prosecute?" Considering the Wall Street banking and insurance debacles, Luther didn't think the government had the resources to go after someone as relatively insignificant as Ira Ripov. Compared to those billions, Ripov was petty cash.

"Not certain," Arthur admitted.

Luther shook his head. How had he gotten into this? He'd worked hard on his book, revised, submitted, been rejected, revised again, was finally accepted and now this. "I think Ira Ripov is doing the same thing to his authors that Simon and Shyster did to theirs. None of us has gotten a penny."

"What's the story of the Lollipop Award?"

"Beats me," Luther admitted. "Maybe Ripov is going to hand out a computer generated certificate suitable for framing, but of no cash value. I wouldn't put it past him."

"That's this evening after the rubber chicken banquet."

"Right. Why don't you interview the other authors? They might know more than I do. You might even find out their real names."

"Will do." Arthur got up to leave.

"Just be careful with Ernest and his elephant gun. It's a real weapon. I've seen the cartridges."

"Maybe he'll use it on Ira Ripov." Arthur, or whatever his name was, moved away.

Luther wondered if "Arthur" was really a detective or a cop.

Twenty-one

When Luther returned to the Ripov Publishing booth he discovered that Caroline had posted the schedule for book signings. He was up first, a one hour stint. There was also a stack of a dozen copies of *Tracking Tenure* and a case of them under the table.

What's more, Caroline was handing out props. Ernest now had, in addition to his elephant gun, a pith helmet, a suitable complement to his book *Safari*. What gimmicks were the others to get? Only he and Ernest were at the desk. The others were presumably circulating, working the crowd like a carload of kids canvassing the neighborhood to sell phony magazine subscriptions.

Caroline produced a mortar board. Where had she found that? "Wear this," she said with a wink. "I couldn't locate an academic gown on short notice."

Luther protested. "I'll look silly."

Caroline moved close enough to him so he could smell her perfume. "Tell the customers your book is a comedy." She set the mortar board cap on his head. "Which side does the tassel hang?"

"Beats me. I haven't worn one of these things since I graduated. I don't think it matters."

Ripov had prepared a nice poster, the book cover and insert of Luther's face, the same publicity picture they had put on the back. Devra had taken the picture, which wasn't bad. Though not a professional photographer, she knew enough to get close and get him to pose.

He dutifully sat behind the display table and put on a hopeful expression, tried to get eye contact with people as they passed the booth, then tried to engage them.

He'd been warned never to autograph anything with the same signature he used on checks. Like some bride who kept writing her new married name to get the feel of it, he practiced a scribble that resembled Luther S--, sort of.

He did no better at selling than on that trip to the bookstore in Newport, on the Oregon coast. Caroline worked the credit card machine. He signed only two copies.

Two copies! He had flown all the way to Miami, weathered the edge of a hurricane, squashed a cockroach in his shoe in the stuffy cabin of a nearly derelict yacht, and sold only two copies. What was his 8% royalty on that? It wasn't 8% of the cover price, which would have been two dollars, but 8% of the wholesale price, less than a dollar apiece. To cover the air fare alone he'd have had to sell five hundred. Was his time worth anything?

He'd read that a book tour costs about a thousand dollars a city. Only someone like Bill Clinton selling his racy memoir could make that kind of sale.

Ira Ripov had told him that though those signings might not produce much at first, he should consider them like acorns that would grow into mighty oaks.

When Ernest's turn came, the pith helmet and elephant gun worked better than that incongruous mortar board hat. Ernest was also a showman. He sold a couple of dozen copies.

Luther hid the detested mortar board cap on the box of his unsold books under the table. For the lunch break, he hoped to get some of the others authors together to talk to them about his meeting with Arthur from *New Week*.

What were their real names, anyway? Luther didn't have a pseudonym. He wasn't writing anything so outrageous that he needed to conceal his real identity. Why else would someone do that? It wasn't as if these were movie stars like Bernard Schwartz who had to assume a name suitable for the marquis of a theater, like Tony Curtis. And they weren't in competition with themselves, shifting to another genre and needing a different persona. Judy Blume would have done better to use a different name when she published *Wifey*, a sexy book for adults, that confused children who were fans of books for prepubescents.

Concluding that the other authors in Ira Ripov's stable were simply eccentrics playing out their fantasies, he snagged Franz and Bram. "Let's get some lunch, a sandwich or something. There must be a McDonald's or other cheap place close by."

But when they got to the street it was impossible to leave the convention hotel. It was simply raining too hard, and blowing. They retreated to the expensive hotel coffee shop.

Franz K-- was uncomfortable. He didn't like crowds, felt hemmed in and intimidated. Bram watched people with suspicion as if any one of them might be a vampire in disguise. He was looking for telltale signs, whatever that might be, and held onto his glittery cross as if he might need to brandish it at any moment.

It was like trying to have a conversation with a couple of nut cases, escapees from a home for neurotics.

Luther's father had once described for him the side show at the Barnum and Bailey circus. Ira Ripov would have made a good pitchman. "Step right up, ladies and gentlemen. See the great attractions. See Jo-Jo the dog faced boy. He walks, he talks, he barks like a dog. And for those over eighteen we have the luscious Fatima... (Caroline in veils and nothing more) as she dances the dance of the seven veils. All this for only ten cents, the tenth part of a dollar..." Except at the Miami fair Ripov was pitching books to independent bookstores, chains, and to the movies, not some yokels off the farm.

Were all authors nuts? Was this a freak show? Luther had thought you couldn't tell authors from anybody else, that they might be like Sally the barmaid at the Port o' Call, people who secretly scribbled down their fantasies like Rawlings in that Edinburgh cafe, or hammered out adventures on an old Underwood portable typewriter like Ernest, but without an elephant gun or pith helmet, just with their fantasies and dreams. Under the tutelage of Ira Ripov with his blazer and captain's hat it was show biz. Step right up, ladies and gentlemen, boys and girls, and buy a book by Ernest H--, big game hunter and adventurer right out of the wilds of Africa... Or see Bram S--, vampire hunter, recently escaped from Transylvania, home of Vladik the Impaler, etc. Did you have to be weird to sell books?

They were nothing so dramatic. Franz K-- ordered chicken soup in a bread bowl, Bram a turkey club salad. Luther's six dollar hamburger was no more impressive than the cheapest McDonalds's 99 cent special but included a small portion of fries. At least the coffee was better than the stuff Mary S-- had found at the donut table.

"I was interviewed by someone from *New Week*," Luther began when they had tucked into their lunch. He told them about the business with S&S publishers.

"We are in the spider's grasp," Bram said, putting down his fork.

Luther felt the similarity. Instead of being rolled up in a cocoon of spider silk they were tied up in clauses and subparagraphs.

Franz, always thoughtful and introspective, said, "Not necessarily. I zink we have recourse. Ira Ripov has made a mistake."

Luther was eager to know. "What's that?"

"Greed is a great destroyer. Do you play bridge, Luther?"

"Not very well."

"But you know zat the two of trump can take a trick."

"Oh? So what's our trump card?"

"I'll tell you later," Franz said, wiping a dribble of soup from his beard. "I don't zink Ripov has counted all ze cards."

Bram looked puzzled.

"Let me put it zis way," Franz said. "Zere are rules to any game. Ripov has broken at least one of zem."

Luther didn't know what that meant but he had his own ideas. "If Ira Ripov is wanted for extortion or fraud or for harboring illegal aliens, he's vulnerable."

"Yes, Luther, but so are we."

Franz wouldn't elaborate.

They each paid their separate checks and went back to the convention hall.

Ira Ripov was working the crowd. It was educational to watch him. He had a fistful of catalogs and bookmarks, told jokes, said he was the captain of the Good Ship Lollipop and his authors were brilliant wordsmiths.

Luther saw him buttonholing a Hollywood producer. Who was it? Spielberg? Luther couldn't be sure. He didn't read *People* magazine or even *New Week*. He wasn't one of those fans who relished all the details of celebrities' lives.

Luther's book was hardly suitable for a Hollywood adaptation. A small independent might find something in it, but nowadays American films were all sex, violence, explosions, car chases, scenes that could be exported and understood without dubbing or subtitles. *Tracking Tenure* had little sex, no bang-bang, boom-boom, violence or stunts.

Would any of Ripov publications fit the movies? Maybe Mary's *Monster*. If a descendent of Cheetah were available, the chimp might be worked into a film version of Ernest/s *Safari*. Tarzan movies were passe, of course. But vampires were in. Bram's book might adapt to a screen play if turned into a chick flick. But Herman's whale book? Hardly.

Of course, Luther hadn't read any of them beyond what stood on the back covers. What did he know?

Luther spotted Herman. He wasn't brandishing his security blanket harpoon, which had been stashed in the booth, and looked lost without it. Unlike Ripov who wasn't afraid to walk up to anyone at all, Herman's defeated, nearsighted demeanor held him back. He wasn't an outgoing, sociable, fraternity type who could walk up, shake hands, and do the "I don't think we've met. I'm Herman," routine. Instead Herman looked like he would do anything to escape, hide in a corner, sneak out to the bar or go up to his room, except they didn't have rooms in the hotel. Their only refuge was back on the yacht which they had left straining at its dock lines in the wind and rain.

Herman was grateful when Luther pulled him aside to ask if Arthur from *New Week* had talked to him.

"Yes, but I couldn't tell him anything he didn't already know. He wanted details of my contract with Ripov Publishing but I told him that was confidential. We have a non-disclosure agreement."

"Maybe even telling him that much is a violation," Luther suggested.

"Has he talked to Mary yet?"

"I don't know. It's her turn for a signing. Let's ask her."

Mary S-- sat behind a stack of copies of *Monster*. Caroline had fitted her out with a doctor's white lab coat, something the might have been worn for a scene in the mad scientist's lair. Unlike Luther, she was doing a fair business. A line of Mary's fans had lined up for autographs, keeping Caroline busy taking payments with the credit card machine. This was no time to interrupt.

Luther would have to wait until they were all together at the same table for what Arthur had called the rubber chicken banquet.

Twenty-two

There was a lull at the end of the long working day to give people a chance to freshen up and change for the banquet. Caroline asked for some help to pack up the unsold copies and the display. Mary agreed to guard Luther's laptop, but Ernest wouldn't leave his valuable elephant gun. Herman sat morosely on a folding chair, fondling his harpoon. That left Arthur, Franz, and Bram to help Caroline load everything on a cart and push it to a side exit.

Where was Ira Ripov? Probably grabbing anyone he could waylay so he could make a pitch for the books. He was like a drowning man, clutching at any opportunity. The Miami Book Fair was a make or break moment for him and it showed.

In *Death of a Salesman* Willie Loman has a speech about a salesman who has a spot on his hat. Once seedy, reduced o begging for a sale, you were washed up. Ira Ripov was out there begging.

If the Crab Cake Marina operator put a lien on the Lollipop and Ripov was evicted from his live aboard office, what then?

Caroline had a rental van in the Miami Beach hotel's adjoining parking lot. There was no underground parking garage, perhaps because, being so close to the Atlantic, it might be flooded by a hurricane surge. As it was, the parking lot was one big puddle, its surface whipped by the gusts of wind. There was actually sea foam blowing across the parking lot.

Holding one of the display posters over her head like a makeshift umbrella, Caroline dashed into the rain to fetch the van and bring it to the entrance. The poster was instantly snatched away by the storm and disappeared.

The wind was howling now, the palm trees bent over. The sound of the waves crashing on the nearby beach was a continuous roar. Hotel personnel were busy securing the furniture around the hotel's swimming pool.

As quickly as they could, Luther and the others loaded the boxes of unsold books and retreated into the hotel.

Time for the awards banquet. The table reserved for Ripov Publishing was at the rear near the swinging door to the kitchen. Luther, with his back to those doors, was afraid if one of the Cuban waiters slipped when carrying one of those heavy trays, the contents might be dumped on his head.

The logo for Ripov Publishing, a picture of the Lollipop, was on a card identifying their table. Candy suckers were at each plate as party favors.

Franz K-- unwrapped his and impishly stuck it in his mouth, looking like a naughty boy who was getting away with something.

The logo for the book fair, a leaping dolphin, was displayed on a banner suspended above the head table. Considering the competitiveness of the publishers represented, a more appropriate symbol might have been a shark.

Ira Ripov had been able to secure a seat at the head table. The seating was arranged so the most important people were in the middle. Ripov was at the end, the bottom of the pecking order.

Caroline wasn't at the authors' table. It was just as well, for her presence as Ripov's assistant and playmate was intimidating. With all the authors seated around a single, round table, they could discuss their successes and failures.

They compared notes through the salad course. The guy who claimed to be from *New Week* had spoken briefly to all of them, but had come away with nothing. In the hopes of reviews Caroline had given away more books than they sold. The book store reps had bags loaded with freebees which might never be given more than a cursory glance.

Some people at the fair were obviously not going to buy anything but came to fill their goody bags. Separating the real from the casual wasn't too difficult. Caroline was adept at spotting the beggars and picking out those who were there to do real business. .

Luther felt no more significant than a face in the crowd. Some of the authors had published twenty or thirty books. He recognized the name of a romance author who had made several million cranking out Harlequin novels. He was not in that class, and not that genre. With only one book to his name he felt he didn't belong.

Turned out, it wasn't a rubber chicken meal. The hotel laid out Red Snapper, a fish Luther never got on the West Coast where salmon and rock fish or mahi-mahi were standard fare. Herman M-- was pleased.

Then they got to the speeches. The state of publishing in a faltering economy was the subject of the keynote, but the speaker tried to focus on positive possibilities, on new trends. The second speaker discussed the attempt by Google to digitize every book for cheap downloads and the class action suit by authors whose work was not in the public domain. It was time for authors and publishers to get together like Napster did for the music industry.

Free downloads were a threat to every author's ability to make a living. Everybody wanted something for nothing.

At one point the lights went out, a temporary power failure that evoked at murmur of alarm among the diners, but they came back on.

People were starting to walk out. Tomorrow was another working day and there we planes to catch.

A somewhat diminished audience remained when Ira Ripov had his turn. Carrying something glittery hardly visible from the back of the room where his authors sat, He took the podium. If he wore a tie under that blazer, the beard hid it. He looked bizarre, like some would-be biblical prophet ready to declare some dire warning about sin and redemption.

Ripov led off with a hurricane joke that, considering the reality of the storm raging outside the hotel, fell flat, then got to the point of his spiel. "This is a great moment for Ira Ripov Publishing. Tonight we're giving out the first annual Lollipop Award. As some of you know, our company headquarters is the great, classic yacht the Lollipop currently stationed here in Florida. To celebrate the success of one of our authors, the one most likely to be a best seller and whose name will be part of the vocabulary of the literary world, I'm presenting the Lollipop Award to MS Mary S--. I see her at our table back there. Come on up, Mary, and get your award."

Mary had left the white lab coat Caroline had provided for the signings back in the Ripov Publishing booth and was wearing a sexy off the shoulder black dress she had packed for the occasion. Hiking up the bosom that threatened to become a costume malfunction, she threaded her way between the tables to the front of the room.

She almost stumbled on the step up to the platform and joined Ripov at the podium. Ripov presented her with the trophy and pulled himself up tall enough to kiss her on the mouth. She cringed, but managed a thin smile before taking the microphone.

"Thank you. The book is *Monster*. I'm working on a sequel."

At their table, Ernest snickered. "What would that be? *Son of Monster? Bride of Monster?* Or *Monster II?"*

Ira Ripov hastened to add, "Soon to be a motion picture!"

So, he had done it. Wrangled a movie contract. Hope was not all lost.

Mary S-- returned to the table with the Lollipop prize.

It wasn't a computer generated diploma, of course, but a small, metal model of a yacht on a stand with a golden lollipop sticking out of the funnel.

"Nice souvenir," Herman said with a touch of envy. "I'd have preferred a model of a whaler, of course."

Franz added, "Should look good on your mantelpiece. Did a check come with it?"

Mary shrugged. "No check."

"I guess that would be too much to expect," Ernest said.

Ira Ripov came to the table, puffed up by his chance in the limelight. "Well, boys and girl, that's that."

Luther asked, "So *Monster* is to be a movie?"

Ripov hesitated. "That's not exactly how it works in Hollywood. We have a three year option If the studio exercises that option they'll pay a fee for the exclusive film and television rights, then hire a script writer to do the adaptation. Of course, they may decide not to proceed, but in any case we keep the option fees."

Mary was curious. "What might the fee be, I mean, if they decide to make the movie?"

Ripov hesitated. "It won't make you rich. If a movie costs ten million to produce and the rights to adapt your book are bought for only forty thousand, you can see that the cost for the studio is a pittance. The star earns more than that."

Forty thousand didn't sound so bad to Luther, who didn't earn half that in a year in his adjunct job at Portland State University. But then, probing his memory of that ubiquitous contract with Ripov, he remembered that the author got only half of foreign translation rights and ancillary rights, which included movie adaptations. And what other charges were there in infamous Hollywood bookkeeping? Kirk Douglas had produced his film *Vikings*, and thanks to the chicanery of the California accountants, ended up with nothing. How much would Mary S-- actually collect, after taxes? "How much do you get on an option? I mean, how does that work?"

"That's between me and Mary, of course," Ripov said, "but typically they'll pay two thousand for the first year, fifteen hundred the second, a thousand for the third."

"So if they drop it after a year, the author's half is only one thousand."

Ripov had to admit, "Yes. But it's a start."

Mary fiddled with her model of the Lollipop. "That wouldn't may my rent for two months."

Ripov forced a smile. "Write more books."

It seemed to Luther that it was precious little return for an author who spent years on a book. You could make more as a greeter at Wal-Mart.

Ripov drew himself up to his full height of about five feet. "We'd better get back to the Lollipop. Jesus should have the car at the front entrance. Do you have all your things?"

Luther had his precious laptop with what few notes he had prepared for his article. This latest bit about the movie contract confused him more than ever. How should he work that in?

Ernest had put the elephant gun back in its locked case. Herman had his harpoon. Only Franz had eaten his table favor lollipop. Luther gathered up the rest to take home to Devra as a souvenir. He'd wanted to shop for something for her, but there hadn't been an opportunity.

Twenty-three

Jesus was waiting for them under the hotel marquis. In the moments it took him to go from the car to the shelter of the canopy he was drenched by the rain. His hair was wet and he swept it back with his hand.

Jesus was morose as usual, his face a model of perpetual unhappiness and resentment.

Ripov explained, "Caroline is taking the books and display materials back to the warehouse."

It was already dark, that quick coming on of nightfall characteristic of the Florida latitude.

They piled in as quickly as they could. This time Luther joined Franz in the luggage space behind the back seat of the station wagon. Mary, her award model on her lap, sat up front with Ripov. Ernest, Bram, and Herman squeezed in the back seat. Like a boat leaving the dock, they pushed off into the flooded streets.

The fake woodie wagon's engine was running rough, as if one of the spark plugs or the ignition had gotten wet as they splashed through the puddles. Luther knew that in six inches of water a car could float and be swept away. Thankfully they weren't fording any streams. It was all standing water.

Lighting came so frequently and was so bright that it shut off the automatic sensors that controlled the street lights. A series of bright flashes would shut them off and they had to be restarted, the mercury vapors having to be re-ignited.

The spectacle excited Mary. "Don't you love lightning? All that unleashed power?"

Nobody agreed.

Luther was afraid the car would stall, the ignition soaked by splashing as they headed back toward Crab Cake Cove. At one underpass they had to stop because the dip in the road ahead was flooded, cars stalled in water up to the doors. They had to detour around it, taking side streets.

At last they pulled up at the marina entrance. The dusk to dawn light was out. The car headlights showed the weather-beaten sign announcing Crab Cake Marina, barely readable through the rain sluicing down the windshield.

Was this a hurricane, or only a gale? As they got out of the car Luther heard the rattle of the tin roof of the shed where he and Mary had caught the wolf spiders. It was coming loose in the wind, the corner lifting. How long would those nails hold?

Jesus, holding his flashlight, led the way to the yacht. The swells rounding the breakwater were more pronounced now, and the Lollipop surged against its spring lines, making the short gang plank slide back and forth like some trick floor in a funhouse. The floating dock was riding higher on the pilings that kept it from drifting away. The seagulls had all flown away.

Was it Luther's imagination, or was the Lollipop riding lower against the dock?

As they each picked their way across, one by one, Luther noticed that everything aboard the yacht was dark. Hadn't Jesus started up the generator?

Luther was glad he'd bought that flashlight, but of course it was down in his cabin. In case they had to evacuate, Luther was glad he had already packed. He could make a run for it on a moment's notice.

There were no lights on in the companionway and it was dark as a cellar at midnight. He felt his way down the steps and, sliding his left hand along the wall, counted doors until he came to his cabin. In the brief flickers of light coming through the leaking porthole from the lightning flashes he was able to locate his flashlight. He unzipped his bag and slid the laptop inside.

Something was missing. He held his breath and listened. The pump was no longer running.

Curious, he found the water tight door that separated the guest cabins from the crew's quarters. He opened the door and, pointing his flashlight into the darkness, looked down into the engine room. There was water down there. What was it, knee deep?

Ripov wanted them to assemble in the dining room, so Luther kept the beam of his flash light at the bottom of the stairs.

A swinging hurricane lantern was suspended over the dining room table. Its yellow light was cheerful, as far as it reached. Before electricity, life aboard ship must have been pretty dark. If you kept looking at the swinging lamp, you might quickly get seasick.

Before Ripov could speak Luther warned him about the water in the bilge. "I think you need to start that generator for the pump."

Ripov gave Jesus a sharp command to get down there.

Luther knew nothing about diesel engines. Did the Lollipop have a bank of batteries? Or did you have to crank up a flywheel or something? What if batteries were immersed in sea water? He had seen *Das Boot*, the German film about a submarine, and wondered if Jesus had to slide on a track underneath the deck and see to the electrical connections. That was the scariest part of the movie.

Jesus, muttering something in Spanish, went below.

Ripov convened the meeting of his authors. "Caroline should be along in a few minutes when she gets back from the warehouse," he said. "I know that you'll be leaving for home first thing in the morning. I want to thank you for coming down for the book fair and for your efforts at making our enterprise a success."

Luther didn't see that it was much of a success, but he waited for Ripov's report.

Maria, looking queasy, stood in the entrance to the galley. She was obviously not used to the unaccustomed motion of the Lollipop in the seaway.

Mary S-- noticed Maria's discomfort and spoke with her quietly in French. What little Luther overheard he couldn't understand. His grad school language had been German, of no use to communicate with Jesus who knew Spanish, and Maria. They disappeared into the galley.

Mary S-- came out, noticed Luther was curious, and whispered, "Maria is pissed off. Ripov hasn't paid her. She threatened to go to the police and he just laughed at her, saying she'd be deported or imprisoned for being an illegal."

Luther nodded. What could he do about Maria's plight? Nothing. He felt like he was a prisoner himself bound up by that damned book contract.

Caroline showed up carrying a briefcase. She peeled off her dripping raincoat. The red power suit she had worn all day was rumpled and damp. "I have those papers for you, Ira."

"Thanks, dear girl. Let's have them."

She handed Ripov six manila envelopes. He noted the name on each and distributed them to the authors. "These are your bills."

Bills? Luther tore open the flap and, to his chagrin, found an itemized list. He discovered that he was being charged for admission to the Miami Book Fair, a portion of the cost of having a booth at the fair, another thirty dollars for the banquet, fifty dollars for the posters advertising his book, and for each review copy of his book that was given out during the event. It was infuriating.

That was not all. At the top of the bill was the paragraph of fine print he had failed to read when he signed the guest list when first coming aboard. Ripov Publishing was billing him a hundred dollars a night for his cabin aboard the Lollipop, ten dollars for each breakfast, fifteen for lunch, twenty for dinner. Coffee was extra, even the glass of champagne from that magnum Jesus had fetched from the hidden wine cellar in the bilge. That ride from the airport was another twenty-five. *What the hell?!*

"I thought we were your guests," Luther protested.

Ernest seethed when he got his bill. "If I'd known this I could have stayed at Motel Six, and they leave the light on for me."

"It's better if we all stay together," Ripov explained.

Bram fingered the cross around his neck, held it up as if to say "Satan, get thee hence!"

"It's an outrage."

The authors looked at each other in joint disbelief and anger.

"Remember your contract," Ripov insisted. "You agreed to pay all expenses related to the promotion of your book."

Luther felt a lump in the pit of his stomach. Even if he did complete the promised article for *Publishers' Journal*, the five hundred collars wouldn't cover all this. "How do you expect me to pay all this?"

"You can apply it as an advance against your royalties," Ripov said with an impish grin.

"So far I've had no royalties," Luther protested. "This is like owing your soul to the company store." At this rate he would not only never make anything on his book, but he'd be in debt forever. "You make Ripov Publishing look like a vanity press."

Franz, who had kept silent, stroked his black bearded chin. "Just one thing," he began calmly. "About our contracts."

Was this the trump card deuce he had referred to?

"What's that?" Ripov asked with a fixed smile and his eyes glittering in the light of the hurricane lamp.

"Under contract law, until money changes hands, ze contract is not valid. You haven't paid me a cent in royalties. I've never got a dime. If you don't pay something, ze contract isn't valid and I can withdraw my book."

Ripov scowled. "Is that your problem? Here's a dollar." He threw a crumpled bill across the table.

Franz refused to touch it.

Ripov wasn't finished. "That law applies up until the work is published. Your book is now in print."

For a moment Luther thought there might be a way out of paying Ripov's bill for expenses. He hadn't been aware of that legal wrinkle.

Franz backed away from his bluff. He had another option. "My contract states zat you will make quarterly royalty reports. You've never sent me any reports and not a penny in royalties. You are in arrears. It's called breach of contract."

"You nitpicking Jews," Ripov sneered. He was angry now. "There's another clause that says if any one part of the contract is invalid, that doesn't negate the rest. You want me to tie you up in binding mediation? You'll never get a penny."

Luther hadn't known that Franz was Jewish, but so what if he was? You didn't have to be a Jew to object to being cheated. "I haven't been paid any royalties, either. You should at least send a periodic report even if there is nothing to report. It's protocol."

"To hell with protocol," Ripov said. "Your contracts are iron clad. When your books sell, you'll make money, but you are responsible for marketing. There's more to this business than merely writing books."

"Writing books is the fun part," Ernest admitted. "Even if I have to do it standing up by an old manual typewriter. Selling books is a pain in the ass."

"I don't think I'll ever see a cent for *Tracking Tenure*," Luther said.

Ripov sneered at him. "So write another book. What are you, a one book author?"

Luther admitted that there were one book authors who made an impact. Walt Whitman's *Leaves of Grass* was essentially only one book, though it went through several versions. It had a profound influence on American poetry. In his more foolish moments, Luther had thought his book, like Dana's *Two Years Before the Mast* had done for seamen, might influence higher education in America, but considering the miserable sales, it looked like it had sunk without a trace.

Bram brandished his cross at Ripov. "You are an evil man."

Ernest wasn't having any of it. "I withdraw my book. You can't have the rights to *Safari*. I'm done with this crap."

Ripov stood to his full height. With his white beard he looked like an evil Moses bringing down the wrath of God from Mount Sinai. "You sniveling bunch of losers. I own you. You are mine. You can't get your books back even over my dead body."

Herman, holding his ever present harpoon, gave Luther a sidelong look and whispered, "Now there's a thought."

Stalemate as the angry authors seethed around the table in the Lollipop dining room. The silent storm inside the room was as menacing as the storm buffeting the moored yacht.

Seeing the menace in the anger he had invoked, Ira Ripov blanched and fled in the direction of his stateroom down below.

Mary S-- fiddled with her award and discovered that the electroplated lollipop that stuck out of the yacht's funnel could be removed. She held it like a dagger. "I'll get that bastard."

Jesus appeared at the door to the dining room. He was soaking wet and wore a grim expression. He looked around for Ripov, but the man wasn't there. Jesus announced to the authors, "Not started. No pump."

Well, Luther thought, *at least the Lollipop is tied to the dock. It isn't going anywhere.*

Maybe not, but at that moment the yacht lurched.

Luther jumped up and went to the door that led to the covered deck. He trained his flashlight on the dock and the mooring lines. One of the spring lines had snapped, allowing the bow to swing a few feet away from the dock. "One of the lines is broken."

Jesus rushed past him and hurried down the deck, held up the frayed end of a nylon line, assessed the situation. He quickly undid the line at the mooring cleat and took the piece of rope with him onto the dock. Perhaps he planned to tie the broken bits together, if the length was adequate.

Luther was alone on the covered deck, braced against the railing. Up on shore Luther saw the flashing light of a patrol car and heard a bullhorn. "Evacuate, evacuate! This is the Dade County Sheriff. Everyone has to go to the nearest shelter immediately!"

Luther needed no second reminder. He shouted to the others, "Let's get out of here." He didn't want to leave his precious laptop behind. Nearly falling in his haste, he dashed down the stairs to the guest section of the Lollipop, found his cabin, grabbed his packed bag, and made for the gangplank upstairs.

He realized he had the only flashlight and handed it to Mary as she stood in a panic, holding her Lollipop award. "Here's my flashlight," he said. "I'm out of here."

The short gang plank, tied at one end to the yacht, had slipped off the dock and hung uselessly, leaving a gap between the Lollipop and safety, but on the next swing of the yacht it crunched against the pilings and he jumped across. He turned back to Mary and the others. "Coming?"

Mary hesitated. She stood uncertainly, holding her Lollipop award in her hand in the shelter of the covered deck. Perhaps she, too, was thinking of getting her things from her cabin. Who knew when they would return? Perhaps never. She went back inside.

"Got to get my stuff," Ernest said, and disappeared down the darkened stairs into the guest quarters.

"Me, too." Herman followed.

Only Luther was prepared for a fast escape. It made no sense to just stand there on the slippery dock in the rain and wind. He headed for the shore.

The headlights of the patrol car illuminated the dock. Luther slipped on the ramp, fell, bruised his knees, got up again, and made it up toward where the old station wagon was parked.

He recognized the black deputy he had met at the Port O' Call, the wannabe screen play writer. He was wearing a yellow storm outfit with a hood. "Where's the shelter?"

"The high school. End of the road, turn left, about a mile inland." The deputy reached inside the patrol car and took a copy of an evacuation map off a clipboard.

The parked station wagon wasn't locked. Luther got in and waited. Where were the others? Why weren't they following him?

At least he was no longer aboard the Lollipop. What if all the mooring lines broke and it drifted off into Biscayne Bay, a dangerous hulk, no lights, a menace to anything it might strike?

Luther opened his cell phone. Devra should be home from the VA by now. The phone screen showed it was charged, but there was no signal. Maybe the cell phone towers were out.

Where were the rest of the authors? What was keeping them?

Twenty-four

The gusts of wind shook the old station wagon. Luther watched helplessly as the deputy got back into the patrol car and drove away. Luther would have gladly followed, but he didn't have the keys to the wagon and he had to wait for the others. Jesus had the key and he was down there trying to reattach the mooring line in the dark, wind, and rain.

Finally, one by one, the five other authors came ashore, breathless and wet from the rain. Ernest carried his gun case. Somehow Herman had been separated from his precious his harpoon. Mary still clutched her trophy, which had lost its metal lollipop. Only Luther had the presence of mind to pack in case of emergency. The rest left their luggage aboard the yacht.

They were followed by Jesus and Maria. The Haitian cook was shivering with fear. Jesus, grim, got in the front seat alongside Luther who handed him the now wet map showing the evacuation route.

"Where's Ripov?"

Ernest explained. "He'll ride in the rental with Caroline. Said he had to get something from his cabin."

"He's not coming," Herman said from the back seat. "A captain has to go down with his ship." He was grinning.

"Serves him right," Franz said.

"What a monster," Mary said with authority. She knew monsters.

Jesus started the engine with difficulty. One of the cylinders was misfiring. Before the station wagon pulled away from the marina they watched as the tin roof of the storage shed blew off and crossed the flooded road right in front of the headlights.

There was no traffic on the flooded roads and they had to dodge fallen power lines, but eventually made it to the high school which was a designated hurricane shelter. The parking lot was full, a disarray of hastily abandoned vehicles. Someone stood at the entrance with a powerful flashlight to guide refugees from the storm.

Jesus dropped off his passengers, but had other plans for shelter. He and Maria drove off into the rain and wind, destination not reported.

In the crowded gymnasium, lit by battery-powered emergency lights, they saw that Red Cross volunteers had arranged folding cots. Underneath the basketball backboard a table had been set up where the six authors added their names to the list of evacuees. A hissing Coleman lantern provided light.

Luther wondered how long they'd have to be there. At least he had his suitcase and laptop. He had his toilet kit and clothes. The others didn't have as much as a toothbrush.

Someone had a crank radio that played the NOAH radio weather reports for a group that crowded around it, eager for news of the hurricane's progress. Gerta was moving inland again, across Florida toward Orlando and Disney World. Winds were diminishing and it was expected that, inland, it would soon be degraded to a tropical storm. There had been several tornadoes and more than fifteen inches of rainfall.

Pulling a couple of cots together for a confab, the six authors rehashed the confrontation with Ira Ripov. "I guess we have to pay his damned bill," Luther said. What would he tell Devra? She hadn't liked that contract, but his book had been rejected several times and he was foolishly willing to sign anything to see it in print.

The other authors exchanged conspiratorial glances. Finally Herman said, "Not if Ripov Publishing goes broke."

Franz, always aware of things legal, said, "In zat case, whoever buys ze assets acquires us as ze accounts receivable."

Mary had another idea. Directing her comment to Luther, she said, "If, for the sake of argument, you understand, Ira Ripov died, we could form our own corporation and buy his assets. That would give us control of our own books."

Herman shifted his weight on the edge of the uncomfortable, folding cot. "Maybe we could buy the Lollipop."

"You must love boats an awful lot to want that albatross around your neck," Ernest said. "I wouldn't be surprised if it sinks at the dock."

"I don't think Ripov owns the Lollipop," Luther commented. "It's probably leased."

"Not if he extorted enough from his old employers, Simon and Shyster," Bram said.

Mary added, "Or from some other scheme. He's a criminal."

They made themselves as comfortable as possible. With the ventilation system shut down and a humidity of a hundred percent, the building soon smelled of unwashed bodies as if they had all been locked in a gym locker full of filthy sweat socks and moldy jock straps. But as long as Gerta didn't blow the roof off, they were safe.

Luther was afraid they might be stuck there for days. Devra was certainly worried, not having heard from him, and until the cell phone towers were back in operation, his phone was useless. It was a harsh reminder of how dependent he had become on technology he took for granted.

He remembered what happened in New Orleans when Katrina drove people into the coliseum. The city water system had failed. In no time the toilets were all stopped up. Diabetics without their insulin could go into coma. There was no ice and the most fragile elderly simply died. Was this going to be their fate in south Florida?

In the perspective of that emergency, Ira Ripov and the Lollipop slowly sinking at the dock were of small importance. Luther could almost put it out of his mind as he concentrated on getting back to Portland. Obviously he wasn't going to make that morning flight and would need another reservation. He was in for an unpleasant surprise.

Twenty-five

They spent two miserable nights in the high school gym. While the hurricane raged around the school a National Guard truck delivered bottled water. One of the evacuees had a crank radio and half a dozen worried prisoners of the storm huddled around it listening for the weather reports. The best the Red Cross was able to muster were loaves of white bread and peanut butter for sandwiches.

On the third morning the evacuees emerged, desperately wanting showers, having slept in their clothes. Luther had fared the best. Though the crowded gym was not amenable to the writer's craft, he'd run down the battery of his Apple laptop working on his piece for *Publishers' Journal*. He hoped Charlie Broadbottom would come through with the promised five hundred dollars. When the low battery warning flashed on the screen he saved the file and shut down.

The school parking lot had not flooded enough to drown the vehicles parked there and the crowd dispersed, families hoping to find their homes intact.

The six authors went separate ways. Luther exchanged email addresses with them but didn't expect to see them again. He still did not know their real names. They stuck to their nom de plume fantasy identities.

Luther bummed a ride with a family of five, a doctor Warshow, his wife Ruth, rambunctious twin boys and an older daughter who rode herd on her young siblings. They were Canadian tourists who'd picked a bad time for a Florida vacation and had to leave their motel when the evacuation order came. The Warshows took him to their Super 8 motel and left him at the desk to register while they hurried to their rooms for a chance to clean up.

There was one room left and he took it. As soon as he got out of the shower and changed clothes he plugged in the chargers for his cell phone and laptop.

Devra would be at the VA and he called her there, working through the automatic system, past the advice to call 911 if it were an emergency, a suicide prevention number, etc. until he could dial her extension.

"Luther! I was so worried. What happened to you? I couldn't get through."

"The cell phone towers were down, power out everywhere. I spent the last two nights in a high school gym but I'm OK. I'm at a motel." He gave her the number.

"Not on board the Lollipop?"

"I wouldn't be surprised if it sank at the dock."

"What about the book fair?"

"That was OK, I guess. But I only sold three copies of *Tracking Tenure.* I'm not a very good salesman."

"What about the award?"

"Mary S-- got that for most likely to be a best seller. She's got a movie deal."

"Wonderful. So when are you coming home?"

"As soon as I can get a flight out. The Miami airport was closed, but I might be able to get something out of Fort Myers if I can get over there." He'd seen power lines down and houses with their roofs blown away, but it was not as bad as the hurricane that literally wiped Homestead houses down to their concrete slabs. If he had to fly out of Orlando or Fort

Myers, how would he get there? "I'll let you know as soon as I have a reservation."

That took many phone calls. Because of so many flight cancellations there was a backlog of tourists wanting to get home. Luther was able to negotiate a change of his return ticket. He hoped he might get a voucher for the motel room because of the delay, but the airline clerk explained that they were not responsible for missed flights because of weather.

Waiting for a flight, he was stuck for two more days, grateful that his credit card was not topped out, and worried that he would have a hard time paying off the bills, not to mention Ira Ripov's ridiculous fees for accommodations on the Lollipop.

The motel was close to a Denny's where he soon tired of the typical restaurant fare: lots of sugar, salt and fat. Country fried steak was a recipe for a heart attack. That was why Devra hated to eat out, not that they could afford it. Even Denny's was beyond their budget. He actually missed the spicy Haitian food Maria served up aboard the Lollipop. He wondered where she and Jesus were. Probably disappeared among the underclass of illegal immigrants.

At least the delay gave him time to finish the story for Charlie Broadbottom and send it by email along with pictures he'd taken with his digital camera. He'd included a sidebar about the Lollipop but didn't mention Ripov's illicit past. If the guy from *New Week* wanted to get into that it was his problem. There was always the risk of a libel suit and Luther didn't want to end up in court with Ira Ripov. The man was too vicious.

Frankly, at this juncture all Luther wanted to do was to get home and put the whole misadventure behind him. He was tired of wearing the same pair of slacks and of washing out his socks and underwear every night. Ira Ripov be damned. When he hit the "send" button for the article it was like typing "the end" to a bad book, or so he thought.

The connections he finally managed to book would take him to Atlanta and, after a four hour layover, a flight to Portland stopping in Denver. He didn't care how many strops it made just so he got home to his wife.

The Motel 8 manager suggested that instead of taking a cab out to the Miami airport he ride downtown to one of the hotels that had a shuttle service. That would save money.

As he got out of the van that took him from the Marriott to the Miami airport terminal, Luther opened his cell phone to call Devra. Though there was a three hour time difference between Eastern and Pacific Time, Devra was already at work. Again he punched the numbers to get through the automatic system at the VA. Devra was busy with a patient, so he simply left a message that he was at the airport and on his way home, would be back in the afternoon. With the change in Atlanta and a stop in Denver, it would be a long day of travel with only pretzels on board the aircraft. He figured he could get a burger in Atlanta.

He left the cell phone on and had hardly got it in his shirt pocket, soiled from several days of wear, when it buzzed. He thought it might be Devra calling back, but the cell phone screen said "unknown caller." Who could that be?

"Luther!"

"Yes."

"This is Charlie Broadbottom. I got your article, but you've been scooped."

"What? What do you mean?"

"*New Week* is reporting that your publisher Ira Ripov is dead. How could you miss that? Some journalist you are."

Luther wasn't a journalist, but he wasn't going to beg the point. "I don't know anything about it. That bastard was alive last I saw. What did he do? Drown in the hurricane?"

"So you don't know anything about it?"

"Nope." Luther was confused. He'd worked hard on that story and it would have to be rewritten with a new slant if it were useable at all. "Does this mean you can't use the story?" If so, there went the promised five hundred bucks. He was still stuck for the air fare to Miami plus the surcharge for having to change the reservation from the cheap red eye to a daytime flight.

Hey, if Ripov was dead, he couldn't collect his bill for accommodations on the Lollipop. Served him right.

"See what you can find out, Luther, but it can't be used in its present form. You're an insider, You must be able to give an authoritative voice to the revision."

"Yes, if I knew anything. I don't."

"Well, put some of that grad school researcher's mind to work. Toot sweet. I've got a deadline to meet." Charlie hung up.

Bewildered, Luther worked his way through the crowd. The airport was mobbed. Some people had slept there on the floor for a couple of days and the place smelled of sweat and dirty socks. There were long lines at the check in. Having no printer, he couldn't print out his own boarding pass in advance, but he punched the numbers on the touch screen, wasn't checking a bag, no extra fee for that, and moved into the line for Homeland Security.

The guard scrutinized his driver's license with a light to determine of it was a fake, but then asked him to wait just a minute.

"Something wrong?"

In a moment he was surrounded by two detectives with FBI ID, stern looks, and ready to draw their weapons if he resisted. The tall one, who was younger, had a shaved head, the smaller a buzz cut with graying sideburns. "Luther S--?"

'Yes. That's what it says on my driver's license."

The taller one identified himself. "Agent Mitchell. FBI. This is Agent Craft. You'll have to come with us."

Craft, clearly the subordinate of the pair, relieved him of his carryon.

Luther pretended ignorance. This must be about Ira Ripov. The guy from *New Week* had said something about Ripov and fraud or extortion. Maybe someone wanting revenge had sent a hit man to take care of Ripov. "What's this about? I'm not carrying too much sunscreen. Security confiscated mine on the way east." It hadn't mattered anyway, for he'd hardly seen any sun until the last day in Florida.

Confused and upset, Luther demanded, "I'll miss my flight. It took me two days to get a reservation."

"You won't be flying anywhere for now, Mr. S--," Agent Mitchell said, and proceeded to read him his rights from a little card, "You have a right to remain silent…" etc.

"I don't know anything about the death of Ira Ripov."

"Did we say this was about Ira Ripov? Is this a confession, Luther S--? Did you kill Ira Ripov?"

"No. I didn't even know he was dead until I got a phone call a few minutes ago."

"Who called you"

"Charlie Broadbottom at *Publishers' Journal*. I did a story for him about Ripov Publishing. He told me Ripov was dead, but now how or when."

"We're holding you as a material witness to the murder of Ira Ripov."

"What? I'm not a witness to anything."

"You were seen at the scene. The deputy who gave you a map of the evacuation route identified you. We have a warrant to hold you for questioning."

"Do I need a lawyer?"

"I suppose you can find one, but that will just delay things. We know you want to get back to Oregon." Mitchell pronounced it Or-ee-gon, not Or-uh-g'n as the natives did. "We just need your statement. We can hold you, of course. Or the judge can let you post bond."

This was all very confusing. "Murdered, you say." Charlie hadn't mentioned murder. Luther would have expected a heart attack or apoplexy from a fit of rage. "I didn't think that wishing someone were dead was a crime," Luther joked. "What happened to that son of a bitch?"

"That's for you to tell us. You'll have to come downtown with us. If we're satisfied with your statement and the judge allows it you can be on a later flight home"

Twenty-six

The agents didn't simply take Luther to an office to interrogate him. They insisted on having him fingerprinted and his mug shot photographed, full face and profile. If he wasn't a suspect or arrested, why did they do this?

The fingerprinting procedures were done in a small room with a full glass window so anything that went on inside could be observed. Luther guessed that was in case the person being fingerprinted attacked the technician.

He had never been fingerprinted before and watched with curiosity as the silent technician, a Hispanic who seemed tired, bored, but wary, inked Luther's fingers one by one and rotated them on the card for the full width of each fingertip. The fingertips done, his hand was held while an impression of all four fingers went into another space on the card.

He asked, "I'm just a material witness. Why all this?" But the technician said, unconvincingly, "It's just routine."

But the man was thorough, even made Luther open his mouth while a swab was taken for his DNA.

Luther tried to smile while his digital photos were taken, full face and profile, but at that point he didn't feel like smiling. He felt like a criminal. Now he would be in FBI files, his information even passed on to INTERPOL if he fled the country.

He reasoned, without convincing himself that all this was just to intimidate him. Agent Craft was tight-lipped, definitely the bad cop of the pair, and treating Luther like a criminal headed for death row was another tool for squeezing the truth out of him.

Luther told himself that he had nothing to hide, that all he had to do was tell the truth. But what if the FBI weren't satisfied with "the truth, the whole truth, and nothing but the truth"?

Luther sat at a table in an interrogation room opposite the two FBI agents, Mitchell and Craft, their tape recorder rolling. As part of the formality Luther was asked to identify himself for the recording and tell his story from the beginning. The agents weren't interested in the restrictive details of the book contracts with Ira Ripov, but they did want to know the names of everyone aboard the Lollipop.

"There's just a crew of two, Jesus who is engineer, driver and deck hand, and Maria the cook and maid."

"That sounds like six people, not two."

"Ripov's too cheap or too broke to hire more than a skeleton crew. But he also has a sexy office assistant, Caroline."

Mitchell seemed to be the senior agent while Craft observed like a kibitzer at a poker game checking everyone's cards and watching for tells, those inadvertent body movements that told when someone was bluffing or lying. "You know their full names? The crew, I mean."

"No. Jesus is a Cuban, illegal, I think."

"That's doesn't help much," the detective said. "Half the Cubans in Miami are named Jesus. It's like Moslems, the men all being called Mohammed."

"Maria is Haitian. Neither speaks much English. They're both undocumented."

"What about the other authors? You say you were all guests on the Lollipop?"

"Well, we thought we were guests. That's the impression we got from the invitation. Turned out Ira Ripov billed every one of us for everything., even a cup of coffee."

"So who are the other authors?"

"Ernest H--, Herman M--, Mary S--, Bram S--, and Franz K--."

"But those are all famous authors."

"Yes, and the real ones are all dead," Luther added. "I think the other authors fancy themselves as reincarnations of the original. It's kind of crazy."

"So what are their real names?"

"I haven't a clue. They all use those pen names and go around acting like they're the originals. They're nuts."

Mitchell was skeptical, as befitting a detective not likely to believe many stories. "You didn't ask them who they really are?"

"Hey, if a guy carrying a double barreled elephant gun with a cartridge like that..." Luther held up his fingers to demonstrate. "....tells me he's the king of Siam, I'm not going to argue with him."

"Elephant gun?" Mitchell and Craft exchanged glances. "Tell us about that."

"Ernest said he won it in a poker game in Kenya. It's worth sixty thousand dollars."

"Have you ever fired an elephant gun?"

"God, no. Ernest said the recoil would knock you on your ass. The shells alone cost a hundred bucks apiece. Who could afford it? "

"So this guy who calls himself Ernest H-- goes around carrying an elephant gun?

"He uses it as a prop for book signings. Dresses in a safari bush jacket."

"Alright. What about the other authors?"

"Herman wrote the book *Whale*. His gimmick is to take a harpoon to his signings."

"Tell us about this Herman M--- and his harpoon."

"He carried it with him all the time like a security blanket. I don't know how he got it on a plane, though I suppose it went in the checked baggage. Come to think of it, when we evacuated the Lollipop he didn't have it with him. We left in a hurry, you see. The Dade county sheriff said we had to get out pronto."

"What about the others? Did they go around with weapons?"

"Not unless you'd consider Bram's cross and garlic weapons. Of course, if you're a vampire..."

"Garlic?"

"Yeh. He had a little sack with garlic. Wore it around his neck along with a big, shiny cross to ward off vampires. I told you these people are all nuts. I'm the only one who doesn't pretend to be someone else. I have trouble enough being myself."

"What?"

"Just a joke."

"We don't joke, Luther."

"So how did you find me?"

"You weren't hard. The marina operator remembered you, and the bartender at the Port O' Call had your signature on a Visa charge. We were slow locating that motel where we just missed you. But you charged your air fare so we waited for you at the airport."

"You could have tracked me by my cell phone," Luther said.

"That was our next step," Mitchell admitted. "We know all about you."

"Then you know I wouldn't kill Ira Ripov. What was he, strangled?"

"Why do you say that?"

Luther remembered the handcuffs on the bed in the master stateroom. "He's into S&M sex. Got handcuffs on the bed posts."

"How do you know about handcuffs on the bed posts?"

"I went down the wrong stairs and found the door to the master stateroom open. There were handcuffs. Then Caroline came out of the shower with Ripov close behind. I excused myself and left. I think he and his assistant take turns beating on one another. How do I know? That's not my bag."

"What's Caroline's last name?"

"I don't know. She never told me. No need to." Maybe next time he was introduced to someone he should ask for a photo ID.

Mitchell seemed satisfied that he now had the persona identified, as least as far at Luther could explain it. "Now tell me what was happening just before the deputy told you to evacuate."

"We were all in the dining room of the Lollipop. There was a big argument about royalties and especially about Ripov's billing all of us for the meals and our cabins on the boat. Can you imagine--inviting someone to your home and then charging them for breakfast?"

Craft broke in. "That would be one way to get my mother-in-law to leave."

Mitchell explained. "Just because you live in Miami all the relatives see you as a place for a cheap vacation. So Ripov actually changed you for accommodations."

"Yes. And then he said that because we'd signed an iron clad contract he owned us. You can imagine how pissed off everyone was."

"Go on."

"Well, Ripov seemed to sense he'd gone too far. He retreated to his stateroom with the authors after him like a pack of mad dogs."

"And that's when you heard the deputy with his bull horn, telling everyone to evacuate."

"Right. I already had my stuff packed. I knew the bilge pump had failed. Jesus said he couldn't get the generator started. The engine room was already flooded and I was afraid the Lollipop would sink. So I just took off. I didn't see what happened next. It was blowing and raining like a sonovabitch. That's when I got the map from the deputy. He's writing a screen play, you know."

"Didn't know that," Mitchell admitted.

"Everybody's a wannabe author. I bet you're planning a novel, too. Or maybe an episode of Miami Vice."

"It occurred to me."

"That's what I mean." Luther was amused. He was surrounded by wannabes. "A word of advice: don't quit your day job."

Mitchell wasn't to be distracted. "So after you got the map from the deputy, then what?"

"I waited in the station wagon. Took a long time. I thought Jesus would never show up with the ignition key. I was afraid the car would blow away."

"The other authors, what about them?"

"They came up the ramp like a human chain, holding hands in case someone should fall into the water."

"How did they act?"

"Act?"

"Yes. Did they behave like they'd all committed a murder, for instance."

"I don't know how anyone who commits a murder acts, You mean, like guilty?"

"Whatever."

"I don't know. But afterwards, in the emergency shelter, they talked about what they might do to get their book rights back in case Ripov died or went bankrupt. He said they could get their rights back over his dead body. I guess that was a mistake."

"So how would they get their rights back? Don't they own their copyrights, or whatever?"

"You'd have to see those contracts yourself," Luther said. "I can hardly understand all the fine print."

"So you think there might have been a conspiracy to murder Ripov?"

Luther shook his head. "I think whatever happened was spontaneous. I wouldn't advise anyone to provoke that bunch of irate, frustrated authors, especially when one has an elephant gun and another a harpoon."

"But you say you didn't see anything."

"No. I just sat in the car, waiting."

"Did you hear anything unusual, like a gun shot?"

"All I heard was thunder and the hurricane about to blow everything away including me."

"And then Jesus showed up with the key and drove you to the shelter."

"Right. That's the whole story. Now can I go now? I think I might still make my flight."

"If you do leave Florida, we may have to ask you back to testify. You can't leave without agreeing to do so. Otherwise we can just hold you here until we have an arraignment and a trial. This can take many months, you understand."

"You mean, in jail?" *What with? A bunch of drug dealers and criminals?*

"The judge can release you on bond."

"Bond? How much could that be?" He was starting to panic.

"That's up to the judge. You have to put up ten percent cash."

Ten percent of what? Ten thousand dollars? Ten percent would be a thousand bucks. He and Devra didn't have that much in savings. No wonder poor people languished in jails even if they were innocent. "I sure don't want to hang around Florida for months. I'd lose my job, such as it is."

"Just what is your job, Luther?"

"Like I told you, adjunct faculty at Portland State University. Part time work. They pay you by the course, no benefits. It's kind of hopeless, which is why I wrote my book *Tracking Tenure*. I thought it might make some money, help the resume, you know. I have a copy in my bag. Want to buy one? Though come to think of it, if Ira Ripov's dead I may never see the royalty."

"What's your wife do?"

"Devra draws blood at the VA lab."

"OK. Now tell me again," Mitchell said. "Why did you come to Miami?"

So he had to tell it all over again. Luther guessed that they were going to compare his stories to see if he'd memorized an alibi. He'd read that people with a cover story memorized it and told it the same way every time, but people who hadn't were inconsistent. Maybe it was a method to wear him down so he'd confess.

Finally he took the initiative. "So tell me, fellows..." He thought if he appeared to be chummy they'd be more friendly. "Just how did Ira Ripov die?"

Mitchell produced a large manila envelope. Before opening it he said, "You were right to expect the Lollipop to sink. In fact, it did, but there was only about four feet of water under it, so it just rested on the bottom of Crab Cake Cove. That was how the harbor master found it when Greta passed over."

Luther remembered. "Ripov owed several months of mooring fees. The harbor master wants to put a lien on the yacht and take possession. Maybe he figured he could salvage the Lollipop, take ownership that way."

Mitchell explained. "You can't claim salvage if the boat's tied to the dock. If it's adrift or ashore on a sand bar, for instance, you have to put a line on it. Then you can claim salvage."

"Oh."

Mitchell continued. "The harbor master put a pump on board and pumped it out, at least enough to get it floating again. Then he went below and found this." Then Mitchell pulled a photo out of the envelope.

The picture showed the master stateroom with its big double bed. There was still water in the room up to the edge of the mattress and a high water mark half way up the wall to show how much it had flooded when the Lollipop sank. In the bed, shackled to the headboard, was the waterlogged corpse of Ira Ripov.

Twenty-seven

Ripov's body had been immersed for a few days. The wild beard was matted. The eyes, open, were clouded over by death and sea water, their impish twinkle gone. The captain's hat was missing, revealing a bald head. Maybe Ripov had been one of those men embarrassed by baldness but too cheap for an expensive transplant or a toupee.

Luther had seen corpses in television news of battlefields but never in such intimate detail, and of course none of those pictures had been of people he knew.

"Take a close look at the picture. What do you see?"

Recovering from the initial shock, Luther narrated his reactions. "Pretty much of a mess. I guess you could expect that. Stuff floats around. I suppose if he wasn't cuffed to the bed Ripov would have floated off someplace. Maybe someone handcuffed him to the bed to let him drown as the yacht sank."

"We're reasonably sure he didn't drown," Craft said, watching Luther and not looking at the photograph.

"What was this taken with? A wide angle lens? Looks distorted."

"There are several pictures of the crime scene. Here's a close-up of Mr. Ripov." Mitchell produced another picture.

"There's something sticking out of the body. My god, that's Herman's harpoon. That must be the murder weapon."

"Not necessarily," Mitchell said.

Studying Luther's face for his reaction, detective Craft said, "Since you're the only one of the authors we've picked up so far, we're like you to come down to the morgue and identify the remains. You have to see the body to get the full effect."

Luther didn't want to look at any corpses. The pictures of Ira Ripov were bad enough. "Is that necessary? I'll miss my flight."

Mitchell checked his watch, a sporty waterproof that looked like it did everything but receive television signals. "You've already missed your flight."

"Didn't the harbor master identify Ripov? I mean, if he found the body. Surely that's enough."

"Maybe seeing the victim will jog your memory. I don't think you've told us everything."

All Luther wanted was to return to the Miami airport to aboard a plane headed west. "Why don't you get the others?"

"We haven't located them yet. You just gave us their email addresses."

"But when they set up accounts for email didn't they have to register, provide that information? You can get it from their internet servers."

"If they registered under their real names, yes, but the way you describe those people, they live pseudonymous lives."

Luther remembered that when he opened his email account he had to provide that information. Registration required agreement to the server's terms, a long legal document nobody read. Luther had, and it included a requirement that the user provided a real name and address, phone number, and date of birth. Most people just clicked on the box that said "I agree." Nothing but their own conscience really prevented someone from lying.

Mitchell explained, "The internet people are cagey about giving out that confidential information. We have to get warrants for each of the internet servers. Takes time. Right now we have you. The other people of interest may have already left Miami. That's why the locals called in the FBI."

Luther felt seriously imposed upon. Didn't these detectives have any sympathy for his situation? They talked about holding him for months. He'd told them what he knew. Could they actually keep a material witness in jail? The school term would begin in a few weeks. Such as it was, he could lose his job. This could be terrible. My god! Luther desperately tried to argue out of it. "Maybe their real names and addresses are on their book contracts. Have you checked the hard drive of Ripov's computer? Looked in his safe? If the Lollipop only sank four feet, the bridge and the office behind it should be OK."

"We'll do that. In the meantime, let's take a little ride down to the morgue."

At least the detectives didn't handcuff him. Crestfallen, Luther walked between the two men out of the terminal. Craft carried his suitcase, which they had not searched.

The only outside indicators that might identify the vehicle parked at the curb as official were a couple of antennas mounted on the roof. Inside, in the back seat, he discovered that, to prevent him from opening the car door and bailing out on the freeway, there were no door handles. He couldn't open the windows, either. At least it wasn't one of those black and whites with bars inside the windows and a grating between the driver's seat and the passengers in back.

In despair, Luther looked out the window at all those free people on the streets of Miami, people who were not in custody. Only about a week before he had arrived to be met by Jesus, that sinister looking Cuban. Then he'd chased cockroaches on board a seedy old yacht, been humiliated by his publisher, and been caught in a hurricane.

He'd seen brochures at the Victoria conventional hotel advertising "the real Florida." He'd guessed that those claims were in response to Disney World at Orlando, which was anything but real. Real or not, Luther was beginning to hate Florida.

What was he going to tell Devra? They hadn't taken his cell phone. He'd wait until he knew something more definite.

Twenty-seven

The FBI car drove into an underground garage. Luther was escorted past security and found himself in the Miami morgue. He was struck at once by the cold and the smell. When Gerta took out the city power, had the refrigeration in the morgue failed, allowing the bodies to putrefy? Or was this the smell of autopsies that opened up the bowels of victims for medical scrutiny? He tried to mentally prepare himself for the worst.

The attendant was a man in his thirties, wearing a surgical mask he'd pulled down under his chin. The name, Solidad, was on the ID tag hung around his neck and embroidered on his lab coat which was stained with substances Luther didn't want to know about. For a person who dealt with death all the time, Solidad was cheerful.

The FBI showed their credentials to the attendant. "We've got a material witness here to identify the body of Ira Ripov."

They were led into a room with a stainless steel dissecting table in the center, shaped so fluids could drain into a bucket below. What looked like built-in filing cabinets lined the walls. Of course, those drawers didn't hold files; they held people.

"Considering that he was under water for a few days, he's in pretty good shape, not like some of the victims washed up after Greta," Solidad explained. "People will go fishing or surfing in spite of warnings. Sometimes we find only pieces the sharks didn't finish. Sometimes we have to identify pieces a shark had in its stomach. You'd be amazed what we find in the stomachs of sharks, even license plates, tennis shoes...."

Solidad found the drawer with Ripov's body. He pulled it open on its rollers, checked the tag on the toe that showed from under the sheet.

Luther was assailed by a smell of bowel and intestines, feces and rot. He tried not to vomit, looked around for something to puke into.

Solidad pulled the sheet from the face of the corpse.

Luther forced himself to look. The beard was unmistakable. There was the bald cranium he had seen in the photographs. If it weren't for the unmistakable beard he'd be hard to identify without that foolish captain's cap. "That's Ira Ripov, all right."

"Show him the whole body," Mitchell said. Craft stood back, watching Luther's reactions.

The body of Ira Ripov in repose looked much smaller on the morgue drawer than he did in life. Solidad didn't uncover the entire body at once. Lifting the beard, Solidad showed that Ripov's throat had been cut, the skin pale on each side of the long gash.

Next Solidad uncovered Ripov's stomach. Under his solar plexus was a gaping, bloodless gash. There were other wounds.

"The wound in the stomach was from the harpoon we recovered, but this is the real cute one," Solidad said, and pulled the last of the sheet off, exposing the groin area.

Luther had glimpsed Ripov's private parts before, the prodigious penis a nearly foot long Italian sausage. Now what remained of the organ hung by a shred of skin. The testicles were gone.

"Looks like he was lying prone when he was shot with a very large caliber weapon. Blew away his business, took the lower spine and surrounding tissue. He'd have bled to death if he wasn't dead already."

Luther remembered the huge cartridge Ernest had shown him at dinner. "Did they find the bullet?"

"Went right through him. Maybe the crime scene crew will find it."

The sight made Luther dizzy and queasy. He shook his head to clear his thoughts. "Probably went right through the hull of the Lollipop. You could sink a boat with that gun."

"What gun?" Craft asked. He'd obviously been waiting for such a revelation when Luther saw the body.

"Ernest's elephant gun."

"Looks like your friends had a party," Mitchell said to Luther.

"They're not my friends," Luther hastened to interject. "I never met them before the invitation."

Solidad showed them three plastic evidence bags. "The harpoon is unusual. The point pivots, so once it's inside the victim it rotates so it can't easily come out."

"That must be why Herman didn't have it with him when he left the yacht," Luther commented. "Kind of stupid, if you ask me. I mean, it's obviously his harpoon. What would he claim, that someone stole it? It's like stabbing someone with a knife that has your name on it and leaving it behind."

Solidad wasn't finished. "We found this shoved down his throat. Garlic. He'd have choked to death on that. And this, I don't know what this is." He held up something golden on a sharp rod.

Luther recognized it. "That's the gold Lollipop off Mary S--'s Lollipop award. It was stuck in the funnel of a model of the yacht."

"Used like an ice pick or stiletto, it was jammed between the victim's ribs. See the mark here?" Solidad pointed it out, a small hole.

"Would that have been fatal?" Luther asked.

"Not right away. When we do the autopsy we'll find out. Looks like it punctured the right lung."

"So you don't know which injury was fatal?"

"Not yet."

Luther was puzzled. "It looks like everyone left their own calling card. Why would they do that? Doesn't make sense. I mean, if I were going to kill someone I wouldn't want to identify myself." Rethinking that, he added, "But then they're a strange bunch of authors."

"Are all authors strange?" Detective Craft asked.

"I think they all have delusions of grandeur," Luther said. "They think publishing a book will make them rich."

"But not you?" Mitchell asked.

"I had hopes, but not delusions."

"So were you in on this little party?" Mitchell asked. "Which was it that killed him, the harpoon in the stomach, the bullet in the balls, the knife in the throat, the garlic in the gullet, or the lollipop in the ribs?"

Luther shook his head. "Or the poker in the library by Colonel Saunders? I haven't a clue."

Mitchell didn't either.

"Whoever was present is an accessory to murder," Craft said. "You say you weren't there?"

"No. I was up in the car, waiting for Jesus."

Solidad was amused. "You'd better pray to Jesus if you were, because you'll get some hard time in the joint for this."

Mitchell: "And Jesus didn't come."

"Not right away. He showed up with Maria, who was so scared she was shaking all over. I thought she was shaking because of fear that the Lollipop would sink with her aboard. Now I think she must have seen the action herself."

"Is that all, gentlemen?" Solidad asked, ready to pull the sheet over the body again.

"For now," Mitchell said.

The body was covered up and the drawer closed. The smell of putrefaction remained.

As they left the Morgue, Mitchell asked, "You have anything to add to your statement?"

"Nothing," Luther said.

"We'd like more background information, just to fill in the blanks."

"You can print out a copy of what I wrote for *Publishers' Journal.* Like I told you, I had an assignment to write a piece about the Miami Book Fair and the Lollipop award. It's on my Apple laptop. Oh, and I've taken a lot of pictures on my digital. You can copy those, too."

"Very cooperative," Mitchell commented.

"Maybe too cooperative," Craft said.

"Hey," Luther protested. "Give me a break. I just want to get back to Portland. Now I have to go through the whole rigmarole of getting a new reservation for a flight."

"First let's have your statement prepared in writing, a transcript of your interview, a copy of your article and your pictures, all signed by you. You'll have to see if the judge will release you on your own recognizance, providing you agree to return to witness at the trial or trials. Then maybe we can expedite your trip home."

"Whatever it takes," Luther agreed. *As long as they don't want a confession.*

"You'd better hand over the camera now. Don't want you to delete any pictures by accident on purpose."

"Sure." Luther handed over his camera. "Let's get on with it."

Craft was apparently satisfied by his observations. "If you still have an appetite after that business in the morgue, I'll buy you a cup of coffee."

"No donut?" Luther quipped.

"That's for the uniforms," Mitchell said. "We do Danish."

Twenty-eight

It wasn't over yet. The detectives left Luther to sit in a hallway with an assortment of strange characters. He had no way of knowing if they were suspects, too, or family members of criminals, or simply derelicts swept up off the streets of Miami. Miami had become a city of immigrants, not just Jews who retired from the candy store in the Bronx, but a new generation, Cubans, Haitians, and others for whom Miami was the New York of the current wave, people who had just enough money to get to America, but not to get further than the port of entry. None spoke English.

Waiting, Luther would have called his wife to give her an update, but there was no signal inside the building.

Hours later Detective Craft called him into an office and asked him to sign or initial every page of a document. On paper his words looked like they'd been spoken by someone else, and they gave the wrong impression, as if he had plotted to recover the rights to his book by means of murder. He read it carefully and insisted on corrections of errors. Any inaccuracy, once signed by him, became evidence that might be used against him. That meant several pages had to be retyped.

Finally, as it was nearly dinner time, he thought he was finished. "Can I go now?"

"Not yet," Mitchell said, looking at his elaborate watch. "While we have you here, let's revisit the scene of the crime before it gets dark."

"What?"

"Back to the Lollipop. You can be our guide, since you know the yacht."

They returned to the garage and headed out. Luther had a chance to see the devastation Gerta had wrought. Trees not blown down had been stripped of their leaves. The shingles of roofs of some houses were peeled off, layer by layer. Signs had been blown away, and the canopies over gas stations askew or knocked down. It looked like Homestead after hurricane Andrew all over again.

Sitting in the back of the unmarked Luther took the opportunity to call Devra on his cell. He got through to the VA hospital lab, but she was on break. He had to leave a message, cryptic and innocuous because he knew the detectives were listening in. Anything he said might be used against him. "This is her husband, Luther. Tell her I missed my flight and will let her know when I get a new reservation."

As they reached the waterfront Luther saw boats blown up on the shore. A couple of sailboats lay like beached whales, furled sails hanging, torn. Except for one, which was sunk, only the cabin top showing above the water, there were no longer any boats tethered to mooring buoys in the cove.

The sign identifying Crab Cake Marina was still there, but the storage shed where Luther and Mary S-- had hunted for wolf spiders was reduced to three standing walls and a pile of rubble.

The Lollipop was bedraggled. The strings of signal flags were gone and the special Lollipop ensign hung in shreds from the yardarm.

A hose led from inside the yacht out on deck. In a pulsating stream it gushed water from inside the hull. The yellow, shore power cable had not been reconnected. After the sinking all the wiring would be suspect. No point in going aboard to be electrocuted.

"You'll need flashlights," Luther said. "It's pretty dark down in the guest room passageway."

The detectives took a couple from the trunk of the car and they proceeded down the ramp, the railings still intact.

A yellow crime scene tape was stretched across the gap in the Lollipop's railing. Inside, the Lollipop smelled of wet wood. The immersible portable pump had been set down in the companionway down below, making a thunderous racket in the long, narrow space. Following the hose from the pump Luther led the way down the stairs to the guest cabins, noticed that the Lollipop still had a list to port and water was trapped along the side of the companionway, a long, narrow puddle caught between deck and the high thresholds of the cabin doors.

Luther pointed out the cabins each author had occupied. "They left in a hurry without their stuff," he shouted above the noise of the pump. "No time to pack when we had to evacuate. I was the only one who left with baggage, so you may be able to identify the people by what they left behind."

"We'll have the crime scene people pick it all up. You just don't touch anything. Evidence, you know."

The water level inside the Lollipop had reached about three feet up into the guest cabins, deep enough to immerse the bunks, but not over the tops of the bureaus. Ernest's old Underwood manual typewriter was still on the bureau where had had left it. The mattress was soaked, of course.

"I see Ernest's old typewriter is still here. I'm sure he'll come back for it."

"An old piece of junk like that?" Mitchell asked, playing the beam of his flashlight on the antique machine.

"It's part of his persona," Luther explained. "Some writers aren't comfortable with computers. There are even some authors who write with a quill pen. I don't think Ernest can write without his old typewriter. He'll be back to fetch it."

"We'd better keep a watch on the yacht to see if the other suspects come back for their stuff," Craft suggested.

Mitchell had another thought. "Since everything down here was soaked, we can have the evidence lab team collect all the personal belongings from the cabins and tell the harbor master if anyone comes looking where they can collect it."

"Sting operation," Craft said.

Luther was glad he had packed his laptop and taken it with him. Once drowned in sea water it would have been useless, all his data lost. "I guess they'll have to throw out all the bedding." Luther commented. "And the cabinetry… what a mess. It'll cost a fortune to restore this."

"I imagine the yacht will have to be scrapped," Mitchell commented, training the beam of his light on the damage. "What's back here?"

"That's the door leading to the crew's quarters and down to the engine room."

They had to step around the roaring pump to get there. The watertight door was open and the intake hose for the pump led down into the bilge. Stepping over the hose, Luther pointed out Jesus's cabin on the left, Maria's on the right.

Above the water level on the wall beside the mirror in Jesus's cabin was a picture of Christ, the only personal evidence in the room. Luther would have opened the bureau drawers, but they were stuck and Mitchell warned him not to.

Maria's cabin was different. On her bureau, above the water line, was a sort of shrine. A plastic Jesus and objects

Luther couldn't identify were arranged in front of the mirror. Luther wasn't familiar with various objects of religious symbolism. "What's that?"

They couldn't all fit into the tiny cabin. "Something Haitian," Craft said, looking over their shoulders. "People come to America and bring their religion with them."

Luther remembered the story of the cruelty to animals law case, about the severed heads of goats found floating in the Miami waterways and the ruling that animal sacrifice was no more cruel than what went on in regular slaughter houses. "I don't think Maria sacrificed any goats, but we did have chicken for dinner."

"Smart ass," Craft quipped.

"Isn't that what a professor is supposed to be?"

Mitchell corrected him. "You're just an adjunct, like you said. Maybe that makes you a dumb ass."

"Dumb to take the job," Luther lamented, "or desperate for work." It was gallows humor, anything to take his mind off the possibility that with the Ripov case he might lose his job. Even an adjunct position was had to get.

Looking down into the engine room they could see there was still plenty of water in the bilge.

"There's a hidden wine cellar down there someplace," Luther said.

"What about the rest of the yacht? Where's the master stateroom where Ripov was found?""

"That's up near the bow," Luther said. "This way."

He led the two detectives back toward the stairs. They had to go up, cross a few feet, and down again.

He could see that beyond the yellow crime scene tape the door had been kicked open, the jamb splintered, but couldn't tell if that had been done by whoever discovered the body or if it had been done earlier.

There was something nailed above the door. "What's that?"

Twenty-eight

This time Devra had accepted Larry Kohn's offer of a cup of coffee in the VA hospital canteen. They sat at a table near the windows among the disabled veterans and their wives who had accompanied them on trips to the Portland specialists. The Portland VA, the largest facility in the state, was the central resource. Vans driven by volunteers brought in patients from primary care clinics around the state.

The vets often wore baseball caps embroidered with the war they had served in or, in the case of navy vets, the names of their ships. Though discharged from active duty, their military service was the pivotal period in their lives, the period of combat that left them lifelong disabilities. Their caps were a badge of honor.

Interspersed among the Vietnam and World War II vets were the new boys and a few women, little more than girls, fresh from Iraq and Afghanistan. It was these new vets that made it necessary for the nurses to screen every patient about symptoms of Post Traumatic Stress Disorder and for the hospital director to include in the recorded message to all callers, "If you are thinking of doing harm to yourself call..." as there had been a rash of suicides among returnees who couldn't make the adjustment from twenty-four hour stress to a peaceful family life.

In that environment Dr. Larry Kohn seemed an anachronism. He wasn't bad looking and had nice eyes, but was a few years younger than Devra. It didn't take her long to size him up. Some kind of a protégé, the young Jewish resident was specializing in urology. Like many young physicians at OHSU he was doing part of his service across the sky bridge at the veterans' hospital. He told her when his residence was over at OHSU he planned to go into research. He had all the earmarks of one of those egotistical doctors who thought they were god and that hitting on nurses was a perk. She was not impressed.

When she got back to the lab to face a waiting room full of elderly veterans still suffering from the wages of war she got the message Luther had left. Why had he missed his plane? She'd planned a special dinner to celebrate his return from Miami. She looked forward to his account of the Miami Book Fair and to learn about the hurricane and the authors he'd said were all strange.

But she couldn't call him back until after work. Maybe when the backlog of blood draws had been worked away…

…

"Don't touch that!" Mitchell demanded.

"What is it?" Craft, standing behind them, asked.

"Got an evidence bag?"

"Right here." Craft handed one over.

Agent Mitchell asked Luther to hold the flashlight while he removed the evidence. It was a makeshift, primitive doll nailed to the door to the master stateroom. Mitchell carefully removed it and slipped it into the plastic bag. He showed it to Luther. "Recognize this?"

It was a crude doll made out of a sock to resemble a little man with a few white hairs stuck in the chin. "Looks like a voodoo doll," Luther said. "It's got a big pin stuck in the chest."

Mitchell had some experience with the occult goings on in Miami. "I bet if the lab analyzes the hair on its chin for DNA it'll match Ira Ripov's."

Craft added, "Probably collected from the victim's hair brush. You have to have something of the person to make these things work, fingernail clippings, hair, or some personal item. This might be one of Ripov's socks. Did Maria also do his laundry?"

"Probably, but I never saw a washing machine. Do you think Ripov saw the doll?" Luther asked. "The power was out. We had that last meeting with the light of a hurricane lamp."

"Maybe not. No telling how long it was on the door or when it was put up there. Maybe he saw it earlier."

"Had to be Maria," Luther said. "Ha! A voodoo curse! Looks like you guys have another murder weapon."

"You didn't make this yourself, did you Luther?"

"Me? I don't play with dolls."

"What about action figures?"

"Not since my mother threw away my GI Joe."

Mitchell shook his head. "Usually we know within minutes who committed a crime. We spend the rest of our time building a case the prosecutor can use for a conviction in court. This one's going to take time."

"Well, you don't have to investigate me," Luther said. "I didn't do it."

"That's what they all say," Craft put in. "Prison is full of innocents."

"Are we done here now?" Luther complained. "This place gives me the creeps. I think it's the smell of waterlogged mattresses and wet wood. Maybe I'm allergic."

"You haven't shown us Ripov's office."

"That's upstairs on the bridge deck."

"We'll follow you."

The bridge deck had not been flooded. It retained its 1930s period furniture with the faded and worn upholstery. Luther showed the two detectives the office Ripov had occupied in what had originally been the captain's quarters. It was still light outside. The low sun shone through the windows. Except for some water stains on the carpet where the windows had leaked there was no sign that the Lollipop had survived a hurricane.

"Remember, don't touch anything," Mitchell warned.

Luther obediently put his hands in his pockets. He wanted to keep his fingerprints to himself. "The safe's open."

It was small, not more than desk high. Whoever had opened the safe that held Ripov's records had left the door ajar. Even without touching the half open door Luther could see that it was empty.

"Did Ripov keep money in there?"

Luther shook his head. "How should I know? I don't think Ripov had any money. His main assets were the contracts he had with us authors."

"Looks like robbery might be a motive," Craft said.

"Who would have the combination?" Mitchell asked.

"Probably his assistant, Caroline."

"The assistant with no last name that you know of."

"Right." Luther was impatient. "She drove the rental van. You can probably locate that pretty quickly, and the rental agency might have her driver's license number on record."

"You should have been a detective, Luther."

"I was a grad student for years. Library research. Sometimes it turns up neat stuff. And don't rental cars have built in GPS locators nowadays to record where the vehicle has been and if it exceeded the speed limit?"

"Some do."

"Then you're wasting your time with me. I've told you everything I know."

Craft said, "We'll be the judge of whether we are wasting time."

"Can we go now? You guys have a lot of work to do to track down all of those suspects. I don't envy you. I bet they all hightailed it in all directions."

"There's no point in holding you here while we look," Mitchell said. "At least we know where to find you."

"Just so you don't pin the murder on me just to get the case off the books," Luther said.

Mitchell smiled. "You wouldn't want that."

"Luther here's seen too many cop shows," Craft said.

"We'll see if the judge will release you on your own recognizance. Then you can go back to your wife and wait."

They left the Lollipop and headed back to Miami.

Twenty-nine

By the time they got back to the city it was no longer possible to see the judge who could release Luther. He would have to stay overnight.

Agent Mitchell was serious. "Luther, I don't think I need to tell you that this was a vicious, brutal crime. For all you know it was a preplanned conspiracy. Whether you were in on it or not, you're our only material witness."

"But I didn't witness anything," Luther protested.

"That's what you say. Let me put it this way: the others don't know what you saw or didn't see. If this is murder one, your testimony can put them in prison for life."

"Murder one?"

"Premeditated. If not premeditated, it's murder two, no death penalty. One thing sure--it's not manslaughter."

"Just butchery," Craft added.

"I don't think it was premeditated," Luther protested. "I think they all just got so mad that they spontaneously pounced on him."

"That's what you think. We don't know that. We have to consider all possibilities."

"Could be a criminal gang," Craft said with menace. "And you could be the next victim."

Luther felt a knot in his stomach. "I don't think so." But the thought wouldn't go away.

"You are an important asset as our witness," Mitchell said. "I think the judge will let you go home, but as long as you are our asset and our responsibility we have to keep you safe."

"How? In the jail?" Luther had visions of being locked up with some psychopath.

"We have quarters for witnesses under protection. That's where you'll spend the night."

The building where they took him looked at first like an innocuous hotel in a bad neighborhood, for the desk clerk was behind bulletproof glass and you had to punch numbers of a combination to call the elevator.

The room they put him in looked like an ordinary hotel room except for the windows. They couldn't open.

"The windows are bulletproof," Mitchell explained, "In case a witness is stalked by a sniper. In your case, you'd better keep the curtains closed. I don't think these panes will withstand a shot from your friend Ernest's elephant gun if he goes after you."

"I don't think he'd do that," Luther said. "I think that big game hunter persona is just an act."

"Bundy looked like a nice, clean cut fellow, but he was a serial killer."

"Yeh," craft said, to reinforce the image. "Those guys who go postal are usually quiet, good neighbors like you. Then go on a rampage."

Luther remembered how often killers were described as quiet men who kept to themselves. Franz K-- and Bram S-- fit that description.

"We'll have dinner sent up to the room," Mitchell said. "And breakfast tomorrow morning. Don't leave the room or the building. I'll come and get you at nine o'clock. Then we'll meet with the judge and see if she feels you can be released."

"Whatever she decides," Craft added, "keep in touch with us. You say you exchanged email addresses with the others.

Don't contact them. Anyone can find out where you live, your phone number. If any of that gang of murderers wants to go after you, it's a simple matter."

"I don't think they're a gang. They're just a group of pissed off authors who never met before the Miami Book Fair."

Mitchell wasn't convinced. "That's what you say. You don't know that. You admit they work under false names."

"Yeh," Craft agreed. "What's the difference if a criminal calls himself Mickey Blue Eyes or Ernest H--?"

Luther thought he knew. "One's a pseudonym and the other's an alias." But the point was moot, a mere semantic play on words that might be appropriate in an academic debate, but not in this case of murder.

"See you in the morning," Mitchell said. "What do you prefer for dinner? How about a nice steak?"

In spite of having eaten no more than coffee and the promised Danish, Luther was too upset to think much of food. "I guess a steak will be OK." He remembered Devra's insistence that he eat balanced meals. "And a salad."

"And pie for dessert?" Craft added. "You look to me like a pie guy."

"Fine. Sure."

They left.

Luther looked at his watch. With the three hour time difference it was still too early to call Devra at their apartment.

Once alone in the room he suspected that there would be surveillance camera all over, that every move made there was watched or recorded. It made him feel like a mouse in a cage surrounded by cats.

He waited until nine Eastern time and speed dialed his home number.

"So when are you coming home?" Devra asked.

"I don't know. There's been a murder."

She was startled. "A what?"

"Ira Ripov, my publisher. It's gruesome. He was shot, harpooned, his throat cut, stabbed, and even cursed with a voodoo doll."

"You're kidding. You're making this up, Luther."

"I'm not. Because I was there on board the Lollipop I'm both a suspect and a material witness."

Devra was beginning to sound convinced. "What's a material witness?"

"I guess it's a witness they want to testify in court."

"Oh."

"But the FBI agents say I may be in danger. They've got me locked up in a witness protection place. I can't leave without an escort."

"So when do you come home?"

"I don't know. But..." The thought occurred to him with a jolt. "The killers may decide to go after me. If you get any suspicious phone calls or mail or packages, be careful."

"Who should I look out for?"

Luther named the authors. "Those aren't their real names. They're all kind of crazy. They use those pseudonyms of dead authors and assume those persona. It doesn't make a lot of sense, but you know how some authors live in a fantasy world. They think the characters they invent are real."

"But they don't just go around killing people." She didn't sound like she believed that herself.

"I wouldn't be so sure. If you assume the role of a monster, how much would it take for you to behave like one in real life? It's like those kids who play violent computer games, then go out and commit mass murder."

"So something set them off?" Devra was sounding convinced.

"Ira Ripov pushed them over the edge. Would you believe-- Ripov charged us for staying aboard the Lollipop, for every meal. He even gave us bills for every cup of coffee."

"What a cheapskate!"

"Yes, but the FBI agents think it's a conspiracy."

"Do you?"

Luther thought about it. "Well, at the hurricane shelter they did talk about forming a corporation to bid for the rights to our books in case Ripov Publishing went bankrupt or Ira Ripov died."

In case? But when they talked to him about it they knew he was dead. It wasn't hypothetical, but they weren't ready to let him know. Had they been planning this all along? Now he wasn't so sure.

The trouble with conspiracy theories was that you began to see them everywhere. Paranoia feeds on itself.

"I'll call you tomorrow after I've seen the judge about getting released."

"You're seeing a judge?"

"I hope to be released on my own recognizance. I couldn't make bail if they wanted it."

"Then what?"

"If the judge demands bail I think they could keep me locked up. Sequestered. Protective custody, I think they call it." He didn't tell her he was already locked in a safe house.

"Really?"

"I don't think they'll do that. I'll let you know. And don't worry!"

"Are you kidding? You tell me a bunch of insane authors may want you dead, but I shouldn't worry?"

"Alright. Just be careful. Don't tell them I'm in police custody. Or maybe tell them I've been arrested for the murder of Ira Ripov." Luther rang off.

The next morning, showered, shaved, but still wishing he had a fresh shirt, Luther was ready on schedule.

They met in the judge's chambers. She was a Hispanic appointee to the bench, important in a community where so many spoke Spanish. A middle-aged, stout woman with a no-nonsense demeanor, she could well have starred in a Spanish language TV version of Judge Judy.

On this occasion Agent Mitchell wore an inexpensive navy blue blazer and a poorly knotted, pearl gray tie.

Luther hadn't asked for a lawyer. Feeling he had no other alternative, he agreed to be available as a material witness if called upon. He didn't want to be stuck in Miami. He knew no one there, had no assets, and sticking around for God knows how many weeks or months would be financially impossible. At least in August the college wasn't in session.

Convinced that he was of good character and not likely to duck the responsibility of testifying should the case come to court, the judge let him go. No bond was necessary. That was a huge relief, like having the handcuffs taken off.

Using his leverage as a government agent, Mitchell secured a coach seat on a through flight from Miami, even persuading the airline to waive the fee for changing the reservation because Luther had missed his original flight. Things were looking up.

In fact, the two agents hustled Luther past airport security. He didn't even have to take off his shoes.

At the check-in gate Mitchell reminded him. "Don't put any of this on your blog or Facebook or whatever internet chats you're involved with. Don't go tweeting your friends about the Ripov murder."

"You sure you don't want me to smoke out the authors?"

"Leave that to us. We don't want to find you with your throat cut or your balls shot off. Just lie low. Pretend to be innocent."

"But I am innocent," Luther protested. They were standing in line at the airport and he was afraid other passengers might be listening.

"So you say."

With his boarding pass in hand, Luther felt a bit more confident. He put a finger on Agent Craft's chest. "You have a way of making everyone feel guilty. I bet your kids are afraid of being blamed for everything." It was just a guess. Luther didn't know if Craft was married.

"My wife takes care of that."

It was best not to bring the worries of work and the attitudes there home with you. Devra never spoke about the VA patients. It was a rule to respect patient confidentiality. Luther wondered what sort of tales were being told about him.

Mitchell gave Luther his business card. "If any of the suspects tries to contact you, let us know right away. Here's my number. Call any time, day or night."

Luther pulled his carryon through the ramp and showed his pass to the flight attendant. He could hardly wait for the plane to take off. It was a huge relief to see Miami dropping away as the plane left the airport. Soon he would be back in Portland.

The murder of Ira Ripov and the collection of mad authors would be behind him. Or so he hoped. But he felt profoundly affected by the whole experience. What had appeared at first to be a junket trip to Miami and a stay on a luxurious yacht had turned into a nightmare. That sight of Ira Ripov's mutilated body... the stink of the morgue... the smell of the wet wood and soaked mattresses raised from the bottom of Crab Cake Cove... He knew his life was changed by those indelible memories. He felt ten years older.

He wondered how much, if anything, of this he should share with Charlie Broadbottom. His piece for *Publishers' Journal* had to be revised. It would be safest to have anything he wrote cleared with the FBI, especially Agent Craft who had a vindictive streak.

Luther arrived at PDX eight hours and three time zones later. He boarded the light rail Max into town. Still shaken, while riding the crowded train he looked at the other passengers with suspicion. How many were drug dealers? Runaways? Hookers? Serial killers? There had been many incidents on the Max, especially in Gresham. The light rail was known to be frequented by drug dealers who took advantage of the free zone, traveling back and forth, making contacts. It made Luther feel as though he were surrounded by criminals. If by coincidence one of the Ripov authors had shown up he'd have been terrified.

He called Devra from the Max to tell her he'd arrived safely and would be home in about an hour. At Pioneer Square, looking around to see if he were being followed, he transferred to a TriMet bus and was soon back at their studio apartment near the PSU campus.

Devra met him with a hug and a kiss. "So tell me about the murder."

"You don't want to know."

"You saw the body?"

"Yes. It was something for your anatomy class. The autopsy hasn't been done yet or I'd have seen Ripov's guts. Anyway, he was mutilated."

Devra swallowed. "You don't have to give me those gory details."

"Honey, if you ever become a surgical nurse you'll see worse."

"Who arrested you? The Miami police?"

"The FBI. I guess because the suspects would have left the state. I'm afraid I didn't you bring any souvenirs of Florida, just some brochures from the Miami Book Fair and a couple of lollipops. I took plenty of pictures."

"No baby alligators?"

"No coconuts carved into Indian faces, either."

She also had a message. "You had a phone call from some Franz K--. He wants you to call him back. Isn't that the same name as a famous author, one you told me about?"

Already? They hadn't wasted any time. "It's a pseudonym. I don't think he even knows who he really is. I'll call him later."

He would have to think about that. If Franz had taken part in the mayhem, there was nothing about the damage to the body of Ira Ripov that pointed to him. The harpoon, the gun shot, the Lollipop stabbing and the garlic down the throat were all keyed to the other authors. Throat slitting looked to Luther to be something Jesus might do. If Franz had been present, he might explain just what had happened, in what sequence.

At the time they evacuated everyone was so tense, excited, and upset by the storm and Ripov's tantrum that he never thought they might be concealing participation in a murder, but then, he'd been out of focus himself, scared by the storm and wanting to get out of there. He wasn't thinking about what might be on the others' minds.

Franz had such a lawyerly, introspective demeanor, Luther didn't think the European would have been an active participant. Franz was an observer who turned his own frustrations into words, not deeds. But then, Franz might fit Mitchell's description of the quiet introvert who kills.

If Luther could draw Franz out he might have something to report to the FBI. How to go about it without tipping Franz off that the FBI were searching for him and the others?

Thirty

There was no telling where Franz was. Best to do some research before returning the call.

Devra had bought a roast chicken at Safeway for their dinner, moist and done to perfection. He was so hungry after the long flight offering no more than a little package of pretzels and soda that he could have eaten the whole bird himself.

As soon as he had supper and changed into fresh clothes, Luther plugged in his Apple laptop and tried building a file on each of the Ripov authors. The trouble was, when he Googled them, all he found were thousands of references to their namesakes. If your name was the same as a famous person, people looking for you would find thousands, even millions of hits.

He tried the Ripov Publishing web site, hoping for links to the authors there, but though their book titles and blurbs were listed Ripov had been too much of a control freak. He wanted his thumb on everything. Links to the authors' sites would give them a measure of independence.

Having made no progress in his Internet search, he checked the screen of his phone to see where the last call had come from. If Franz had not called from a public pay phone, he might still be at that number.

Luther was in luck. Franz picked up on the third ring. "Luther, how are you?"

"How'd you know it was me?"

"I haff caller ID. So you are back in Washington?"

"Oregon. Where are you?"

"I am still in Florida."

"What about the others? Where did they go when they left the shelter?"

"Back to ze Lollipop, I zink. Zey were all in a hurry to get out of Miami."

"I can imagine," Luther said.

"Did you go back to the yacht?"

Luther didn't want to lie. "Didn't have to. I had my stuff, remember? I was the only one who left with his belongings, except maybe Ernest. He had his elephant gun."

"Zen you haven't been in touch with Mr. Ripov?"

"No. Haven't talked to him. That sonofabitch."

"Ja. He vass an evil man."

Was? Past tense. "Do you think he'll ever pay us any royalties at all?"

Franz was firm. "No."

Luther puzzled over how he might broach the subject. "Are the others still interested in forming a company to buy back our rights if he goes bankrupt or, er… dies?"

"Yes. Zat is a possibility."

"With your background in law, maybe you could look into it. Set something up, like a partnership or something."

"Ja. Zere are limited partnerships and somezing called an 1120S corporation."

"There you go." Luther could see a possibility for getting the authors all together for a corporate organizational meeting. Then the FBI could pounce on them all at once. "Would you all get together to sign papers, or something?"

"Not necessary. Zey could do it by telephone, fax, or email."

"Are the others all still in Miami?"

"No idea. I zink zey all vent in separate vays."

That wasn't so good. If they were all in touch with each other and the FBI arrested one, the others would be warned and disappear. Their arrests had to be coordinated. "Did you go back to the Lollipop?"

"Ach, Luther. I'm afraid the boat sank while vee were in ze shelter."

"I was afraid of that," Luther said. "The pump wasn't always working. If the power went out, which it did, the yacht would take on water. And in the hurricane...."

Franz still hadn't said whether he knew Ripov was dead. How could Luther broach this? "I didn't tell you that I was writing a piece for *Publishers' Journal* about the Miami Book Fair and Ripov Publishing."

"I didn't know. Did you write about all of us?" Was there worry in Franz's voice?

"Yes. My friend Charlie Broadbottom gave me the assignment. Then he told me I was scooped by *New Week*." Luther hesitated. Should he reveal what he knew? How could he put it? "There's a report that Ira Ripov is dead. Do you know about that?"

Franz was silent.

"Franz? You still there?"

But Franz K-- had hung up.

Thirty-one

Just to be on the safe side of the law, Luther immediately called Agent Mitchell's number to report on his conversation with Franz K--. "He's still in Florida," Luther said, "but didn't tell me where."

"What about the others?"

"No idea. You might get hold of copies of their books. Sometimes the blurb about the author says where they live. Mine says I teach at Portland State University."

"We'll track them down," Mitchell said.

Luther remembered the sight of the body of Ira Ripov and all those wounds. "What do you think actually killed Ripov? I mean, any of the wounds could be fatal."

"That's up to the coroner to report. There's an autopsy. It's made difficult by the fact that the body was under water for a couple of days. It wasn't found until the harbor master put a pump on board the Lollipop."

"Then Ripov might have drowned in his bed." Luther had an image of Caroline handcuffing Ripov to the bed and leaving him there as the yacht sank. She didn't strike him as that diabolical, but you never knew.

"I don't think so, but being immersed like that makes it difficult," Mitchell admitted. "I'm no coroner, but I do know that dead men don't bleed. If, for example, you stuck the harpoon in him when he was already dead he wouldn't bleed. If there was fresh blood, the sea water might just wash it all away. It's going to be quite a puzzle."

That was something Luther hadn't thought about. Stabbing a dead person wasn't murder. It was, what did they call it? Interfering with a corpse? Cutting off some body part as a macabre souvenir after death wasn't the same as murder.

In that case, only the person who dealt the killing blow was the murderer. The others might be co-conspirators, participants in a felony.

Was it the same as charging the driver of the getaway car for murder in a bank robbery where a guard was killed by another of the gang? Luther would have to study up on criminal law. And of course, each state had its own laws. He remembered that the penalty for rape in Florida was death, but in other states rape might get you a few years in prison, but not death.

So what was the penalty for "interfering with a corpse"? And if conspiracy couldn't be proved in court, how would the Florida prosecutors frame their case?

It was like one of those cheap "who done its." Just so Mitchell and Craft didn't include him in the sweep.

Mitchell wasn't through. "Did Franz K-- give you his phone number?"

"No, but my phone keeps a log of past callers. Just a second."

Luther read off the number.

"That a cell phone?" Mitchell asked.

Luther hadn't thought about it. Franz could have called from anywhere--a hotel, a cellular phone, whatever. He didn't know the area codes for Florida. If Franz had called from a land line that would lead the FBI to a specific place. He didn't think Franz had used a pay phone, for he would probably not have been near it to take Luther's call back. When a cell phone was turned on the relay towers triangulated its location. Otherwise they couldn't make a connection. "I don't know. If it is, you can track him down."

"We'll find him. My partner Craft is like a bloodhound. Once he gets a scent there's no stopping him."

"What about the autopsy?" Luther asked, curious. "Any way I can find out what actually killed Ira Ripov?"

"You don't need to know that," Mitchell said. "Leave it to the prosecutor and the court."

"I suggested that Franz might get the other authors together to form that corporation to bid on the rights to their books. Franz says a gathering isn't needed. Any other way to get them all together so you can arrest them all at once?"

Mitchell thought about it. "They might come to pick up the stuff they left behind on the yacht. Some criminals do unbelievably dumb things."

Luther suggested, "Why not put them in the Marina office as lost and found and have an agent there to wait to see if someone shows up to make a claim. "

"That's a thought."

"Ernest might come back for his typewriters, but I don't know if the others brought anything with them that they couldn't just abandon. Credit cards or checkbooks, maybe."

"Someone could send a courier, pay some kid five bucks to go claim their stuff for them. It's what we call a cut out."

"Oh." Luther felt compelled to find some way for the FBI to satisfy the need to make an arrest, just so it wasn't him.

Mitchell was thoughtful. "I'll see if we can set up a sting to lure them all in."

Thirty-two

"What are the FBI going to do?" Devra asked. She had saved all the bones and the carcass from that Safeway chicken to cook up for soup. She put the bits in a large stainless steel pot along with a cut up onion and some celery tops she'd saved.

"How should I know? I'm not an FBI agent. They must have resources."

Devra was skeptical. "Maybe this will become one of those cold cases."

"They have plenty of suspects. Me included."

"You?"

Luther shook his head as if to clear his thoughts. He was putting their dishes in the dishwasher. Their studio apartment didn't have a real kitchen. It just had a galley and a space big enough for a table for two. If he could ever get a full time position maybe they could afford a one bedroom, but rent in Portland was high. "They call me a material witness. I think it's an excuse to keep me on a leash."

"What if this Franz guy, or whatever his real name is, says you're the killer? The whole bunch of them could say you murdered Ira Ripov. It would be their word against yours."

Luther hadn't thought about that. There were plenty of stories of innocent men sent to death row by false testimony. If those crazy authors lived in their pseudonyms, what was another untruth? He didn't want to be part of their fantasy world. Why did he have to go to Miami anyway and get involved in all this? If it hadn't been for Charlie Broadbottom's promise of five hundred bucks for the story he'd have had a legitimate excuse to stay home. Certainly the non-existent royalty income from his book didn't justify his effort. Unfortunately, the contract he signed stated that he had an obligation for advertising. Ripov could have insisted that Luther go to Miami at his own expense.

Luther knew Ira Ripov was a pain in the ass to deal with, but who would have suspected he'd actually charge his authors for accommodations on board the Lollipop when he'd invited them himself? That was a miscalculation on everyone's part. Talk about chutzpah.

And now he was playing the part of police informant. He told himself he didn't have any choice, that he had to cooperate or risk being arrested for the crime himself. That Craft fellow was capable of it, Luther was sure. Who could be more diabolical? Ripov or Craft? Power was a game they both played and he, Luther, was in the net.

So now he was in effect denouncing Franz K--. What if Franz were innocent? He always struck Luther as meek, withdrawn, but not as weird as the others. Having an aversion for cockroaches was something Luther could easily relate to. Franz also seemed engrossed in the law. Probably it was one of those Jewish things, all those speculations and nitpicking about the Torah. That could put you into a perpetual state of indecision.

Herman with his harpoon was like a neurotic kid who still goes around with his baby blanket or his pet teddy bear. Maybe that harpoon was some kind of phallic symbol for Herman, a weapon that gave him a macho feeling of power, like those NRA guys with their bumper stickers, "You can take my gun when you pry my cold, dead finger off the trigger." To Luther that stuff was evidence of subconscious sexual inadequacy.

And Mary S- what about her? A nature freak. Luther remembered her standing in the thunderstorm, risking being struck by the lightning that actually did hit the power pole. "Isn't nature wonderful?" She said she felt like dancing naked in the rain. He'd have liked to see that. And then hunting spiders, not what one would expect from a woman. Spider hunting--that might be OK for little boys, wannabe big game hunters but looking for bugs instead. Mary was a bit twisted, too. She looked normal enough, but to write that book *Monster* took a creepy imagination.

And as for creepy imagination, Bram had to be the winner. He'd been so immersed in his vampire book that he saw them everywhere. Luther didn't think it was just an act. Bram, walking around with that big cross and the pouch with garlic around his neck, really was nuts.

Ernest in his safari outfit was the real macho man. Of course, he could have made up that story about winning the elephant gun at poker. It was like those wannabe big game fishermen who buy a stuffed marlin at a garage sale, hang it on the wall at home, and make up a story about how they caught it.

The trouble with all this speculation was Luther didn't know what to believe. He was caught up in his own musings. Being worried about having to go to court to testify and maybe reaping the revenge of the suspects didn't help.

So now he was a police informant. At what point did cooperating with the FBI turn him into what crooks used to call a stool pigeon?

He hadn't lied to Franz. He just hadn't told him all he knew. He didn't tell Franz he had seen the mutilated corpse of Ira Ripov.

It was best not to interfere. Luther had the email addresses of all the suspect authors but Mitchell had warned him not to contact them. Best to stay out of it. Put it behind him. Go about his own business as if nothing had happened.

As for his book, *Tracking Tenure*, that was a lost cause. He should never have written it. The idea of getting rich on an academic novel was a pipe dream, and he didn't even smoke.

The only people who made any money in the book business were the publishers and distributors. Not that Ripov seemed to have made any money except maybe by extorting something from his previous employer. The independent bookstores were going broke. Too often the big publishers miscalculated, printed overruns that ended up remaindered at Cosco or Wal-Mart or on the bargain table at Powell's. There you could buy a remaindered twenty-five dollar hard cover for less than a cheap paperback. Did authors make anything on those?

Luther concluded that he'd earn more as a greeter. "Welcome to Wal-Mart!" At least that paid minimum wage and you didn't have to pester someone like Ira Ripov for some piddling royalty.

He should never have thought of being an author in the first place, and now he was an FBI stooge who could be risking his life if the suspects wanted revenge.

Luther resolved to do nothing.

The question was, was it too late? At least Portland, Oregon was thousands of miles away from Crab Cake Cove and the derelict yacht Lollipop. He could go back to the mundane business of being an underpaid adjunct at PSU hoping to some day be full time, if not at PSU at one of the many colleges around Portland. Reed or Lewis and Clark were too prestigious, but PCC or Pacifica might hire him.

Then when Devra finished her nursing degree she could move up from being a med tech at the VA and the two of them could buy a condo or a house. He could forget about that menagerie of crazy authors. Or so he hoped.

Thirty-three

A couple of anxious weeks went by. Luther was occupied with preparations for the fall term at PSU. He got no strange emails, no more phone calls from Franz, no contact with any of the authors and no word from the FBI. It looked like Luther might have escaped the whole nightmare.

He thought that maybe the murder of Ira Ripov had turned into a cold case, that the FBI had been unable to locate the other authors or Caroline or Jesus or Maria and the murder of Ripov would be lost in the shuffle of Miami murders that were easier to solve. What was one mysterious death when there were drive by shootings, gang wars, international drug cartels, and much other big fish to catch?

Surprise: he got a notice that he had registered mail, return receipt requested to be signed only by the recipient. Since he wasn't at home when the mail was delivered, all he got was a yellow slip of paper that said he had to pick up registered mail at the University branch post office.

The Portland University branch post office was a short bike ride from their studio apartment near the PSU campus. As usual, there was a long line of customers waiting to be served by the two clerks on duty, people with multiple packages and would be travelers needing to file their passport papers. The wait only added to his suspense and anxiety.

When his turn at the window finally came Luther presented the yellow notice and asked, "Who is it from?"

The clerk, an Asian woman who was always friendly, had no comment. She probably had to hide that information in case a recipient refused to accept the mail, a problem that only meant more paperwork. "I need some photo ID."

He got out his Oregon driver's license and showed it.

"Just sign here, please."

He signed the receipt and was handed a manila bank envelope, the kind used for sending documents. Luther retreated to a counter and amidst the supply of postal blanks for insurance, forwarding notices, and special mailings, tore open the flap.

It was an official-looking letter from a law firm in Miami and full of lawyerly language. On the twentieth off the month at ten AM his presence was requested at the law office for the reading of the will. Ira Ripov's estate included him as one of the beneficiaries. The stipulation was that all recipients had to be physically present to collect.

At first Luther was relieved. Maybe Ira Ripov had a conscience after all, a loyalty to the stable of authors he claimed to own. Maybe the royalties had been accumulating in an escrow account. Or maybe, as in a bankruptcy hearing, he was included among the creditors.

Luther had never been, to his knowledge, in anyone's will. His parents were still alive. He had no relatives in Florida. He had not reached the age when the older generation was dying off, rich uncles or aunts leaving surprise sums to surviving nieces and nephews. Nor had he been a claimant in a bankruptcy case, trying to collect unpaid fees for an article published by a magazine that went under without paying an agreed upon sum.

He knew nothing about all that legal stuff. He couldn't imagine that any piece of Ripov's estate would justify the expense of another round trip flight to Florida, hotel bills, meals, etc. Jesus wouldn't be picking him up at the airport for a ride that turned out not to be free after all.

He had begun to realize that *Tracking Tenure* was a worthless book. That Ira Ripov hadn't paid any royalties didn't necessarily mean that the publisher was cheap or miserly or a cheat. It meant that nobody wanted his book. He might, one day, find a copy among the deleterious of the Goodwill store.

Did he want a piece of that derelict yacht? That would be a white elephant, indeed, a hole in the water to throw money he didn't have. In accounting terms, pursuit of whatever Ripov's estate had to offer was not cost effective.

He did not want to go back to Miami.

There were other options. Maybe the authors had formed that corporation they'd talked about in the hurricane shelter and wanted him in on their scheme to divide the spoils of the dead Ira Ripov.

Maybe Ripov had a life insurance policy that named his authors as beneficiaries. That was possible. At least Luther did know that if you killed someone for their insurance money you could not collect. That meant that the irate authors who in the fit of their insane rage murdered their publisher could not collect anything but a lifetime lease on a Florida cell, what prisoners called three hots and a cot.

Luther resolved not to go to Miami. Life insurance, estate, escrow royalties or not, he did not want any part of any kind or anything to do at all with Ira Ripov Publishing. He was through. Finished. Done.

Except he'd better call Agent Mitchell to keep him informed, as promised.

"Ah, Luther," Mitchell said when he answered his phone. "What's up?"

"I got this letter demanding my appearance in a law office in Miami."

"So you got it. Good. Be there."

Silly me, Luther thought. *I should have known. The whole thing's a setup.* "What's it about?"

"The sting operation you suggested."

"I didn't suggest a sting operation."

"Yes you did. It was a good idea. But you have to be there."

"What? I don't want to go back to Miami. I'm done with this."

Mitchell's friendly voice was no longer friendly. "You made an agreement with the judge. You will be there. Do I have to send a US Marshall to accompany you in handcuffs?"

"Wouldn't that cost the government a lot of money?"

"The government spends forty grand a year to keep one worthless drug user off the streets. What's a couple of days of US Marshall's time compared to that?"

Luther remembered his deal. If he hadn't made it Agent Craft had threatened to keep him in custody until a trial. True or not, bluff or otherwise, Craft could be convincing in his bad cop mode. "Alright. If you provide the air fare I'll come willingly and save the government the wages of a US Marshall and his per diem."

"That's more sensible, Luther. Go down to the Portland FBI office and pick up a government travel voucher. They'll be expecting you. You can turn it in at the airport for a ticket. As soon as you make the reservation you call me and either I or Agent Craft will pick you up at Miami International airport."

That sounded reasonable. Maybe he could have a couple of days vacation at government expense and see Miami, actually make use of the bathing suit he'd brought along to the Lollipop but never wore.

There was more. "We'll have to keep you sequestered until the meeting in the law office. And you are not to contact anyone about this or you'll blow the whole operation, understand? If you warn off any of the other authors I'll have your ass for obstructing justice."

Hopes of sunning himself on the Atlantic beach faded. "Can I fly first class?"

"Don't push it, Luther. Even I travel coach."

"No limo from the airport?"

"You're a comedian, Luther. I've read your book. Well, at least parts of it. You'd do better writing comedy."

"After all this I don't think I'll write another book. It's too dangerous."

Mitchell agreed.

It wasn't only publishers who might be crooked. Agent Mitchell must never know who was legitimate. Even the Laundromat where you took your clothes might be a front for criminals to launder money. Mitchell's world was full of crooks, drug dealers, terrorists, and other disreputable. No wonder the man was suspicious of everything. What a life.

Thirty-four

"I have to go back to Miami," Luther told Devra when she came home from the blood lab. He showed her the letter from the law firm.

"You think the Ripov estate owes you money?"

Luther didn't want to tell her it was a scam to lure the other authors in. If she got a call from Franz, Ernest, or the others she might accidentally give it away.

He never lied to his wife or anybody else. Lies only led you into more lies which had to be backed up. The truth needed no fabrication to remember. How could he dodge this one? "The FBI insist that I be there."

"Oh."

"No further comment or explanation needed," Luther said. "If Franz or anyone else calls, I'm off to Miami to see some lawyers. End of story."

Devra wasn't satisfied. "Is it dangerous?"

He hadn't told her the grisly details of what he'd seen at the morgue, only that Ripov was murdered. He hadn't told her that the windows of the room he'd been sequestered in were bullet proof, but maybe not strong enough to stop a shot from Ernest's elephant gun. Best not to worry her more than she already was.

Luther rode his bike in the rain down to the FBI office in the government building on Third Street. At the entrance, which was blocked off by concrete barriers to keep back some Timothy McVeigh truck loaded with explosives,

Luther had to empty his pockets, go through a metal detector, and "do the airplane thing" as the cautious guard requested, his arms out like wings while the wand was passed over him. He was pronounced clean, picked up his stuff, and found the FBI office.

Even that had additional security. The receptionist in the small waiting room was behind bulletproof glass. It was a different world, indeed. Did Mitchell and Craft live in daily danger of being blown up in their office? No wonder Craft was so tense and hostile.

Luther slid his driver's license under the gap in the window. "I was told to pick up a travel voucher."

"Got any other picture ID?"

He guessed that drivers licenses were so often bogus that they weren't trusted. "Just my faculty ID at PSU." He dug that out of his wallet.

His ID was returned and he was told to wait.

Eventually a suspicious, tall agent wearing a pistol at his belt came out of the inner office with a file folder. Without showing Luther the contents the agent compared his face with a document inside. It probably had Luther's mug shots. Satisfied, he handed over a blue card. "Just show this to the travel agent. You can use it on any airline."

"Thanks."

He had been drawn further into the coils of law enforcement, unfamiliar territory for a mere adjunct faculty member who lived in a world where everybody, well, almost everybody, was innocent and law abiding. A little more of this and every night he'd be looking under his bed for evil doers.

When he left the government building he waved to the security guards who had searched him, like he was one of the insiders himself. Did they sense his new role as one of them?

Back at the apartment, he phoned the airline for a reservation and it wasn't difficult, even though the airlines had cancelled flights to save money and substituted smaller planes so as not to fly half empty. Mention of the government voucher, that he was traveling at the request of the FBI was like a ticket to the VIP room.

He notified Mitchell of his scheduled arrival time and got his carryon suitcase out of the storage locker in the basement of the building. It still had the tags from his last trip. That seemed to be from a long time ago, a bad memory best forgotten. But of course, he couldn't forget.

The morning he was to leave they left the apartment together, Devra to get the #8 bus up to the VA, he to get the MAX light rail out to the Portland airport for the early flight. Devra asked, "How long will you be gone?"

"I don't know. Day or two. Might be back tomorrow."

"It's a long way to Miami."

He kissed her as they parted company at the bus stop. "Clear across the country."

"Be safe," she said.

"You, too," he said. "And watch out for those needle pricks." There was a hazard when dealing the lab sharps. Some patients had hepatitis or were HIV positive.

"Always."

So he was off. It was going to be a long day.

Thirty-five

When Luther presented his blue travel voucher card to exchange for a boarding pass at the Portland airport he was surprised. The clerk, a dark-skinned, wrinkly, middle aged woman of undetermined race, looked up from her computer screen. "The voucher is good only for one way."

Panic. "But I made a round trip reservation."

"Your voucher only pays for one way."

"How am I going to get back?" Was he to be stuck in Miami? Did the FBI plan to hold him there until a trial, or whatever? This was damned unfair. He suspected it was Craft's doing. The Agent liked to toy with him.

"You can pay for that portion of the trip yourself or take that up with whoever issued the voucher," she said.

"I guess I'll have to ask the FBI for the return." He didn't want to pay for the flight himself and then play try and collect with the government.

"Are you checking any bags?"

"I just have a carryon." He slipped it into the gap in the barrier and she attached a baggage tag.

"You have to take it over there to be inspected."

As he followed her instructions he was worried and distracted. Why did they give him a voucher for only a one way ticket? Would they issue another for the return to Portland? Or was this just another leash to keep him from chickening out?

He watched as the Homeland Security staff in their latex rubber gloves opened his suitcase and rubbed it with pads that would indicate whether he carried explosives. They took out everything Devra had so carefully packed for him, saying that guys never knew how to pack. Certainly Homeland Security didn't care if his clothes were jammed in and emerged as bundles of wrinkles. They would be now.

His seat was in the last row of the plane jammed up against the bulkhead so it couldn't be tilted back. He tried to sleep, but just as a cabin at the bow of a ship gets the worst of pitching and rolling, the last rows of a plane swing back and forth like the tail of a fish. He was glad to find a barf bag in the seat pocket in front of him, even though he didn't have to use it.

Neither Mitchell nor Craft were at the Miami airport to meet him. Instead, a young, friendly agent spotted Luther, showed him his badge. "I'm agent Shebelski," he said. "This way." Shebelski took Luther to an unmarked car waiting at the curb under the watchful eye of an airport policeman who nodded when they arrived. This time Luther got to sit in the front. It was one of those cars with lots of electronics, radio, GPS, and a shotgun in a carrier convenient to the driver.

"Where's Mitchell and Craft?" Luther asked.

"At the law office organizing the team."

"I imagine it's a complicated operation, making sure all the suspects show up."

Agent Shebelski nodded.

"So what happens? When everyone shows up they get arrested at the same time?"

"That's the plan."

"Then what do you need me for? I'm just a material witness."

"You can identify them. But you don't go in until they're all there and you don't say anything."

"All right." In a way, Luther was looking forward to it. Might be exciting, as long as there were no violence. He wondered just what was done to stage the sting.

Shebelski drove to a bank building in downtown Miami and they took an elevator up to the tenth floor. A man dressed as a custodian was at work in the hallway. He nodded to Shebelski and continued to pretend to be working. They approached the law office of Lye, Chete and Steele, a firm Luther recognized from the Car Talk radio show on Public Broadcasting. Somebody was having a joke.

A pretty brunette in a maroon business suit loose enough to conceal a holstered hand gun was the receptionist. She told them to go on in.

It was a conference room with a marble-topped table so big it must have been hoisted up to the tenth floor on the window washer's crane and passed through a window to get it in. On a sideboard was a coffee urn, Styrofoam cups, and a tray of for what to Luther was a telltale offering of Danish pastry, no donuts. There were chairs for at least ten people. A lawyer-looking man sat at the head of it with an open briefcase in front of him.

The Ripov stable of authors had arrived, all the suspects. Luther was impressed. Well, there they were. Not everyone. Caroline wasn't there, nor were Jesus and Maria.

Luther greeted them all. Mary S-- was wearing the same black outfit she'd had on at the book fair but with a little matching jacket to cover her shoulders. She looked expectant, like she was finally going to collect something for her book *Monster*.

Franz K-- looked troubled, but then he always did. Herman M-- in his thick glasses looked a bit forlorn, probably missing his harpoon. He should buy or make another. Ernest H-- was uncomfortable, looked resentful but that was probably because his back was so bad he preferred to stand. Bram S-- wore his cross as usual and had replaced the garlic pouch with another.

They were not the only ones in the room. Agents Mitchell and Craft were also there, sitting up against the wall near the door with a couple of other alleged bystanders.

The man posing as the lawyer representing the Ira Ripov estate didn't waste any time. "I'm Dan Steele," he said, "representing the interests of Ira Ripov. I have good news for you and bad news. I don't know if you'll think this is good news or not, but after a great deal of trouble the autopsy performed on Ira Ripov shows that the cause of his death was a heart attack brought on by a stroke. Ira Ripov had previously had a quadruple bypass and was in poor health. None of the injuries inflicted on him by those of you who are present actually caused his death. You cannot murder someone who is already dead."

At this point Steele looked closely at the authors in turn. Then he continued. "That's the good news. Except for Luther S-- here, who I see is present, you are all under arrest for the desecration of human remains. The bad news is that mutilation of a body is a ten year felony."

Agent Mitchell then took over and, taking out a little card from his wallet, recited the familiar Miranda warning, "You are advised that you may remain silent..." et cetera.

"A heart attack? What was he, scared to death?" Luther asked, incredulous.

Agent Craft spoke softly to Luther. "Possibly. Would you believe that voodoo doll? Obviously Maria, the Haitian woman, nailed it to his door. Remember the strange religious stuff we found in her cabin?"

227

"I thought Ripov was superstitious, never going without his captain's hat. He was a nutty as Herman with his harpoon."

"What would you do if someone nailed a voodoo doll to your door?"

"I don't know."

"Power of suggestion," Craft explained. "That combined with what you told us about what happened at the meeting when you were all presented with bills for meals and accommodation. All those angry authors must have frightened him."

"But you haven't arrested Maria."

"We haven't found her yet."

"Do you think a jury would convict her of murder by voodoo?"

"Not bloody likely, unless the court finds a jury consisting of Haitians. She'll simply be deported."

"Then it wasn't a conspiracy," Luther said. "They were just so angry they went berserk."

"Seems so," Craft agreed.

"But then they may all get off on a plea of temporary insanity. You think a jury will convict?"

Craft shrugged. "It's up to the prosecutor to bring the case to a judge and jury. Fortunately, in this country no one person acts as the one who arrests, tries, and convicts. It's my job to apprehend the perps. The rest is up to prosecutors, judges, and juries."

"Then you've seen some guilty parties get off."

"I'm afraid so. We do the best we can to provide prosecutors with adequate proof of guilt. If we can't make a case, yes, some get off."

"But you know who they are."

"Yes, and once a criminal, usually they do some other crime later and we get them on that."

Luther remembered that often someone who was only a suspect in a rape case was tracked down and found to be already in prison somewhere else on another charge.

Would Mary, Ernest, Franz, Bram, or Herman kill some other publisher in the future? Who knew?

Would a jury be convinced by a defense argument that Ira Ripov deserved to be shot, stabbed, harpooned, choked, and have his throat slit even after death? Were there extenuating circumstances? Was it justified mutilation? Or would lawyers call it temporary insanity worthy of only probation or community service, perhaps warning groups of wannabe authors of the dangers of writing books? People in crowds tended to go crazy, and this neurotic bunch of authors who lived in their pseudonyms were already half cracked.

"But what about Franz?" Luther asked. "Franz didn't do anything."

"He was present, as he has admitted. Franz has turned state's evidence. The most he'll get is the thanks from a judge and maybe some community service for not reporting the incident right away."

"Oh." Leave it to Franz K-- to find a legal loophole to wriggle through.

"And by the way," Agent Craft added. "Franz backs up your story. You didn't see any of it happen. You're off the hook."

So the FBI believed that neurotic, cockroach obsessed Franz K-- and not Luther. Thanks a lot.

Except for Franz K-- and Luther the Ripov authors were taken in away in handcuffs.

As they parted company, Franz said to Luther, "I told you zere vass a vay out of ziss."

After they all left the law office, Luther asked Agent Mitchell, "Can I go home now?"

Mitchell smiled. "Looks like it. With Franz acting as state's evidence, your role as a material witness is moot."

"So do I get a voucher for a return flight?"

"We'll take care of it."

"Think there's time for me to spend an afternoon at the beach? I brought my bathing suit."

Mitchell advised, "Just remember your sunscreen."

Epilogue, six months later

To: Charlie Broadbottom, Editor
Publishers' Journal
Park Avenue
New York, NY

Dear Charlie,

Thanks for the check and for publishing my story of Ira Ripov Publishing and the Miami Book Fair.

The trial is all over, at least as far as the Ripov crazy authors are concerned. Except for Franz K-- they all got fined, a year's probation, and community service. No sign yet of Jesus or Maria.

The FBI tracked down Caroline, but that case isn't resolved yet. I guess she's the one who handcuffed Ripov to the bed which may have contributed to his heart attack. Who knows? You just never know who to believe or what the real facts are.

The harbor master at Crab Cake Cove has a lien on the good ship Lollipop for the unpaid mooring fees and plans to turn it into a party boat if he can ever get it dried out.

The authors did get together and form a corporation to bid on the Ripov Publication assets, but the whole package got bought up by Liechtenstein, the conglomerate that bought out Simon & Shyster. I suspect they wanted to get hold of anything Ripov had in his possession from his mischief at his old employer. Unfortunately, the package included the rights to all our books and we are bound by those contracts. Liechtenstein's people have no interest in selling our books and are in effect suppressing them. They have no interest in me, either, and have waived their rights to first refusal on my next book, if any.

I suppose any copies of *Tracking Tenure* that are out there are now rare collector's items.

I don't know if I will ever be foolish enough to write another book, but if I do, maybe I'll call it *The Lollipop Murder*.

Good luck in your career in New York publishing. It's a dog eat dog world. Frankly, you have my sympathy.

Your old roommate,

Luther S--

If you enjoyed *The Lollipop Murder*, you may like *The Gold Chromosome.* Here's a sample:

The Back Story

Gold was not our mother's original family name. It was something Russian and, unless you're a Slav, unpronounceable. Great grandfather Isaac, so the family legend goes, had the chutzpah to steal a horse from a drunken Cossack and flee to Poland. He kept running westward and landed in England where he settled among the Russian Jewish immigrants in London's east end. I think he had a push cart -- no horse-- in Petticoat Lane where you're likely to have your pocket picked.

Great Grandpa's having stolen a Cossack's horse seems to have set the pattern for the whole family, for though they may not be horse thieves, the Golds are brassy, conniving and crooked sometimes even criminal.

Great Grandpa Isaac had several children but only Abe emigrated to America. Times were always tough in the East End, so as soon as Abe could he got a steerage passage to the United States. His first act upon arrival at Ellis Island was to change his name to Gold. He'd heard that in America the streets were paved with it, and he wanted to get off on the right foot.

Grandpa Abe Gold was only fourteen, claimed to be sixteen, and got to Chicago where he started as a runner, carrying numbers for gangsters. Eventually Abe had his own news stand in the Loop. Until I learned the true nature of grandpa Gold's business, I always wondered how someone could move from Hyde Park on the South Side and retire to such a fine house in Deerfield and drive a Cadillac on what he earned selling copies of the Chicago Tribune, the Sun Times, and a few magazines.

Abe Gold married and had six children, all of whom grew up while the family still lived in Hyde Park. Ann Gold Rottman, my mother of blessed memory, was somewhere in the middle of the brood and Sadie was the youngest. Naturally, there are lots of cousins. Those were the days before television and birth control. Besides my mother and Sadie there were...well, let me get to that later. I'll introduce them as we go along, and I guarantee you won't be disappointed. Trust me. Trust-- that's a family joke.

Chapter One: Sitting Shiva

You know how it is with funerals. Relatives who are seldom in touch and may not be on speaking terms gather to pay their final respects. Sadie was the youngest of the Gold family, one of six children on my mother's side, the last of her generation. She made it to her ninety-third birthday, had a stroke, and that was it, dead.

Some of the cousins still live in the Chicago area and my home is in Michigan. Not everyone made it to the funeral. My brother Harold refused. Not that he had anything against Aunt Sadie. He didn't want to be in the same room with the cousins, even for a funeral. When our mother of blessed memory was dying of cancer, none of the cousins showed any interest. They didn't come to her funeral and had the chutzpah to ask if they were in her will. Harold never forgave them.

Those who did show up for Aunt Sadie's funeral gathered in Sarah's cluttered living room. So there we were, I, my weird sister Sarah, and three other cousins at Sarah's crazy apartment in North Hollywood.

The funeral people had provided Sarah with a Shiva candle, the kind that burn for the seven day period of mourning. We're not Orthodox, so we don't spend seven days in darkened rooms in our stocking feet with the mirrors covered. Others are supposed to bring in food so you don't have to cook while you contemplate the loss of your loved one and say prayers.

There was a silent moment while we watched Sarah light the Shiva candle and set it on the mantelpiece to celebrate or mourn the passing of Aunt Sadie.

Cluttered is a euphemism. Sarah may be pushing sixty but she never got over the Raggedy Ann doll stage. She has hundreds of those rag dolls piled everywhere in her apartment, staring with those blank, trusting, painted on black eyes, enough to fill a museum.

She even dresses like Raggedy Ann, wears her hair in braids, though her braids are gray, and wears an apron and red and white striped stockings. Sarah's eyes are gray, too, unlike Raggedy Ann. Sometimes she has that blank look like Dan Quayle.

Sarah never goes anywhere without one of those damned dolls. It's her obsession. There's a miniature Raggedy Ann dangling from the rear view mirror of Sarah's Lady bug orange, vintage Volkswagen. Look in her commodious shoplifter's purse and I'll bet there's a Raggedy Andy hiding in there. It's her dream to sell her collection to the Getty Museum for a million bucks and retire. She has two problems with that: 1) she could never part with those dolls and 2) the Getty Museum is interested in real art. A possible third reason is that there's already a Raggedy Ann museum in the Midwest.

Aside from trading in dolls, Sarah used to almost earn a living photographing bar and bat mitzvahs. Videographers do that now, preserving the proverbial "today I am a man" speeches forever on videotape. Sarah has an aversion to such newfangled media, asserting correctly that they are not as archival as her own black and white prints. Trouble is, no one wants black and white still photos of bar mitzvahs these days.

She is not averse to computers and the internet, and is forever trading on eBay, searching for that rare doll not yet in her collection and sometimes selling off the duplicates. She buys and sells under the pseudonym Mamadoll. Memorabilia is her shtick. Collecting is her disease.

Our older brother Harold is her benefactor. Collecting dolls and taking bar mitzvah pictures doesn't pay the rent. Harold does. "She my baby sister," he told me once, even though, like I said before, she's almost sixty.

Gathered in Sarah's cluttered space to mourn Aunt Sadie, you wouldn't know Sarah even had a computer, for it was almost buried in the dinette under a pile of staring dolls.

So there we were, the five cousins who made it to the funeral plus one spouse, gathered at Sarah's place, comparing notes about Aunt Sadie, the last of her generation. Making it to ninety-three means good genes, not necessarily good quality of life. Her life had ended, but not her story. For me, it was the beginning.

As for the late Aunt Sadie, whom I hadn't seen in years, my recollection was of a fragile old lady with blue hair and a limp. I do remember that she had a reputation of never picking up the check at lunch. There's a story of her trying to take home the carcass of a thanksgiving turkey in a doggy bag when she visited my mother, she should rest in peace. Imagine asking to take home not just a doggie bag, but half a turkey! Sadie had that Gold chromosome: chutzpah. That's how I remember her. It's a one-sided memory at best.

"She had a tough time of it in the end," my sister Sarah said as she passed around a tray of Mogan David HD wine for a kiddush blessing. That Raggedy Ann apron and striped stockings made her look like a waitress in some theme restaurant, not our hostess. "I couldn't get her to pay her bills. She'd just put them away in a drawer."

I took a glass of wine. "Too cheap to pay her bills? Sounds like Sadie."

"No," Sarah corrected, looking at me from under her unkempt, gray bangs, "Just didn't want to be bothered. Didn't want to sweat the details. That's why I was given power of attorney. I took over paying her bills. Didn't want her phone to be cut off. Not that she made any calls herself. If they cut off her phone, how could I reach her?"

My cousin Schmuel, schlemiel to my mind, took a glass of wine off the tray and chugged it down before we got to the blessing. He's one of those Californians who wears his sunglasses indoors. At least they're plain dark, not the asinine reflective kind. Schmuel got his start standing on street corners hawking maps to the homes of the stars. Later he sometimes worked as an extra at Universal so considers himself part of "the industry." In California that means the movie business, what else? Schmuel licked his lips. "So you got power of attorney. Who set that up?"

Sarah was reluctant to say. She took a deep breath, looked away, and admitted, "Harold."

Schmuel gave us both a suspicious look. "Your brother the lawyer? How convenient for you."

"Nobody else in the family was willing to help her out. She told me that when she needed someone to take her shopping you were always too busy."

Schmuel shrugged. "I got business to attend to. So what about Sadie's estate, since you're privy to inside information? Any money there?"

"Yes," his wife Sylvia put in. Some people would call her Schmuel's trophy wife, but to me she's just a braless dyed brunette shicksa who married Schmuel thinking he had money because he drove a Lexus. Schmuel has a thing for expensive, flashy cars. Maybe Schmuel did have money once, before he lost it in one of his schemes or Sylvia got hold of his credit cards. "So are we going to inherit?"

Sarah wasn't saying.

"I bet she had plenty," Schmuel said. "She never spent any of it." He paused to reflect. "Those jokes she'd tell! You're never believe the language that came out of her mouth."

Up to now my cousin Millie was quiet. Millie lived a couple of blocks away from Sadie's old apartment on Fairfax. Millie's husband had been self employed but never paid any income tax, so when he died his social security didn't help Millie much. What little money he left her got eaten up by Millie's medical bills years ago. Like Sarah, she lived on food stamps and was lucky to be in rent controlled housing. She didn't drive, never owned a car. As a widow Millie supplemented her social security by working part time at a Good Will store as a cashier. That explains why everything she wore was no longer in style. Millie's wardrobe was the opposite of Schmuel's wife's. Sylvia wears stuff manufactured with the labels on the outside for status.

Cousin Millie agreed. "We were crossing Fairfax once when a driver tried to drive through the zebra crossing with her in it. Some guy with a big Mercedes. Sadie whacked a dent in his hood with her cane and when he got out of the car to confront her she told him he was a stupid motherfucking Nazi trying to run down old ladies in the crosswalk. 'Piss off before I call the cops!' she said. You should have seen the look on his face. The guy fled."

I never expected modest and self-deprecating Cousin Millie to come out with language like that, even quoting Sadie. This family is full of surprises. Whacking a Mercedes with her cane? Clearly that wasn't the Aunt Sadie I knew, but then I didn't know her. I live in Lansing, Michigan, thousands of miles from LA, so had no opportunity to protect drivers from Aunt Sadie's mouth or her cane when crossing Fairfax.

Schmuel had done Sadie's memory the honor of putting on a shirt with collar and sleeves as a sign of respect. Not the usual California style where tee shirts, shorts and sandals are the uniform. By contrast, Jake Gold, my cousin from Chicago, was the only one who came to the funeral in a suit. Jake, a little guy with a paunch, wore a navy blue, pin stripe, three piece Italian business suit to give himself a look of respectability and shoulder pads to make him look bigger than he is. Fortunately, the shirt wasn't black and the tie not white satin like you might expect on someone like him. His shoes looked like they were elevated to give him a couple more inches.

What you notice about Jake is not what he wears, but how he wears it. Jake has a sort of swagger, the demeanor you see in cops and police detectives, or on made Mafia men. There's no proof, but it's common knowledge in the family that Jake is a gangster. We all know that "Mafia Man" Jake is the only one in the family who, like our late Grandpa Abe, has a news stand in the Chicago Loop. Same business and it ain't just newspapers and dirty magazines. Jake said, "If you think she had a foul mouth, did you ever play cards with her?"

None of us had. I had heard Sadie played fan tan with her pals in the nursing home where she lived the last two years of her life, but I had never played cards with her myself.

Jake had more to tell. "I used to play casino with her when I was a kid, before Uncle Dave was killed and she moved to LA. She'd cheat."

"Cheat?" my sister Sarah asked.

"Yeh." Jake was still holding his full glass of Mogan David HD. "Are we doing a blessing or what?"

We all raised our glasses, praised God and thanked Him for the fruit of the vine and drank to Aunt Sadie's memory.

"Eat something," Sarah insisted. She had put out a tray of distressed bagels that had languished for God knows how long in her freezer. She had smeared them with a little cream cheese, but nobody wanted to eat the proceeds of Sarah's food stamps.

Jake returned to his story. "Imagine cheating a little kid at casino. She had this dishonest streak."

What did Jake care about dishonesty? "Runs in the family, maybe?" I said, remembering the family history.

Jake didn't smile. He gave me one of those looks meant for people who deserved to be dead, soon. "Ever know why she moved to LA? How Uncle Dave came to be killed?"

I searched my memory. Family business gets pretty complicated and the stories blur. Each time they're told someone embellishes the truth for greater effect. Maybe the stories blur because they're just rumors and malicious gossip. "No. I think he was in the used car business."

Jake returned his now empty wine glass to Sarah's tray. His fingers hesitated over a little dish of candy hearts with the caption "I love you" just like the hearts in the chests of Raggedy Ann and Andy. Jake popped one in his mouth and talked around it. "Used cars is a euphemism. Dave was in the hot car business. He'd get a few stolen

Caddies, forge the bills of sale, and sell them on time payments at high interest to the schwarzes."

Schwarze is no longer politically correct Yiddish. The translation is "black" but the negative connotations are the same as "nigger."

"Dave knew the schwarzes could never keep up the payments, so when they'd miss he'd simply repossess the cars and sell them again to some other suckers." Jake paused, crunched the candy heart and swallowed. "One day one of his customers got lucky. Won big in a back alley crap game, and came in with a buddy to pay Dave off in cash. Wanted the title to the car. Dave didn't have a title."

Now Jake had a tight circle of cousins all listening, rapt. It's a long way from Chicago to LA. Schmuel's wife Sylvia, for sure, hadn't heard this story. I hadn't, either.

Jake gave us his humorless smile. "So Dave takes out his gun, kills 'em both, puts them in the trunk of the Caddy, and drives it into the canal by the old steel mill in Gary." He chuckled. Obviously to Jake killing schwarzes is funny.

I knew there was something shady about my uncle Dave's car business, but I didn't know it involved murder. There was more.

"Everything was OK for awhile, but some of the schwarzes' friends from the crap game knew they were headed for Dave's car lot and got suspicious. He'd bumped off the wrong guys. So one day when Dave doesn't show up for supper and doesn't answer the phone Sadie drives down to the South Side to see what's up and finds him all tied up, dead. They cut his throat."

"What a shock for Sadie," I said. "Must have been a sight."

Jake caught my grimace. "That ain't the half. First they took down his pants and gave him a second circumcision. They cut his cock off."

I shuddered at the description. "You sure they weren't Arabs?" I asked. "Sounds like something Arabs would do." I remembered stories of Arabs cutting off a victim's penis and stuffing it into his navel, which I guessed was making someone into a motherfucker. Obscure acts of symbolic mutilation elude me. I'd have to ask Deborah, my wife the psychologist. She'd know. "So Sadie left Chicago and moved to LA," I said, thinking that was the end to the story.

"Not Sadie," Jake said, his expression cool and tired. "First she put out a contract on the guys who did it. As payment she handed the business over to the people who furnished the cars and split."

The amazing thing about this story wasn't that Sadie had put out a contract for murder, but that my cousins weren't horrified or even much surprised. Maybe we live with so much murder and mayhem that we're no longer shocked by anything. Deborah would call it a double standard, that the cousins would have been upset if the victims were Jewish, not black.

I doubted the story. "How do you know all this?"

This time Jake's smile was genuine. "Some of my business associates are familiar with the details."

Schmuel complained that Sarah had provided no better than Mogen David, but refilled his wine glass anyway. "I thought you Mafia types took the code of silence."

Jake shrugged. He had unbuttoned the vest of his three piece suit. "It was a long time ago. The principals are all dead. Besides, this is family business." He nodded at Sarah's four walls.

After waiting patiently for a break in the conversation Millie spoke. "I always thought Sadie was a sweet old thing. I used to go over to her place for coffee. I'd get some day old pastry at the deli and we'd sit on the balcony and visit. She knew everybody. She also never forgot if you did her wrong. She had a grudge against the landlord, but that's a long story I won't go into." She paused as if considering whether the next subject was appropriate. "So are we going to inherit anything? She lived so poor, there can't be anything to her estate."

Sarah had told me that when Sadie moved into the nursing home she had phoned Millie and given her Sadie's microwave, television, coffee pot, and what remained of the better dishes. A few possessions and some worn out furniture wasn't much of an accumulation after ninety years.

Sarah hesitated, not knowing what to say or if she should say anything at all.

Schmuel insisted. "I hear Sadie left a chunk of money. Who gets it?"

Sarah collected the empty wine glasses and put down the tray before she explained. "Sadie's assets were put into an irrevocable trust. Harold set it up."

"Dear cousin Harold," Schmuel said, his voice dripping with suspicion. He looked at me. "Why didn't your brother come for the funeral?"

I could have said my brother Harold is too fat. At over three hundred pounds he has to fly first class or they can't wedge him into a seat on the plane. "Got a big case," I explained. Harold is the oldest of the Rottmans and the brains of our side of the family. His law practice is in Indianapolis. Mom was a Gold, of course, but she married a Rottman. Considering the prejudice Jews of German extraction hold against Russian and Polish Jews, marrying a Rottman was a step up in the world. Of course, being Rottmans doesn't mean we didn't inherit the Gold chromosome.

Sarah relented and explained. "Too bad he couldn't come to the funeral to explain all this himself. That legal stuff is beyond me. I do understand that you're all to get a few hundred dollars as a token."

Schmuel was puzzled. "What about you?"

Sarah was embarrassed. "The interest from the trust fund goes to me while I'm alive."

"And then?" Schmuel asked, licking his lips and looking at her over the top of his sunglasses as if to assess how soon her demise might be.

"Then it's to be split among the cousin, I think."

Schmuel was counting. "That's us in this room, Harold, crazy Arthur in Calumet city, and his ditsy sister what's her name?"

"Miriam," I said. "The one married to a butcher with the two kids."

Sylvia wasn't counting relatives. She was figuring how long Sarah could live before she died and the rest of us divided up Sophie's estate. She protested. "We could all be dead by then!"

Jake shrugged. "You never know." To Sarah he added, "You got life insurance?" It sounded like a threat.

Sarah didn't take it as a bad joke. "For who should I buy life insurance? Who would collect? Raggedy Ann and Andy?"

Schmuel checked out the collection. "Make me your beneficiary. I heard this stuff is valuable. These must be worth a bundle." He picked up a doll from the pile that cluttered the couch.

"Hands, off, Schmuel."

I could feel the tension rising in the room. The Gold cousins. Not a pretty lot. Maybe it's a good thing we're not close.

So that was my reintroduction to Aunt Sadie: a little old lady who wouldn't spend a penny, who drank coffee with cousin Millie on the balcony, Sadie who cheated at cards, wasn't afraid of drivers who encroached on zebra crossings, and was capable of putting out a contract for murder. Next time I see a little old gal with blue hair, tennis shoes and sunglasses with rhinestones I'll give her extra respect. Maybe that's why the street thugs never grab their shopping bags. Hit a bag lady and you're soon dead.

. . . .

The Gold Chromosome is offered as an ebook download from Wings ePress and as a paperback at wwwl.lulu.com.

About Harley L. Sachs:

Though born in Chicago and raised in Indiana, Harley L. (Luther) Sachs considers himself an international, having lived in Germany, Sweden, Scotland, and Denmark. He earned a degree in English at Indiana University, then served in the US Army in Germany. After getting his Master's degree at I.U. he returned to Europe and worked under cover for several years. He met and married Ulla in Stockholm, Sweden and they spent a year's honeymoon in a Scottish castle. Returning to the USA, Sachs taught English briefly at Southern Illinois University then moved to Michigan Technological University in the Upper Peninsula where he and his wife raised three daughters. He took early retirement and lives in Portland, Oregon.

Harley L. Sachs is the author of many novels, short stories, magazine articles and newspaper columns. His short stories have been broadcast on the BBC World Service short wave and on Oregon Public Radio's Golden Hours. The web site is www.HarleySachs.com.

Here's a list of books by Harley L. Sachs:

MYSTERY NOVELS

The Mystery Club Series

THE MYSTERY CLUB SOLVES A MURDER

First and most popular of the Mystery Club series. Mary Higgins finds
the body of Dora Reed on the roof of the Plaza retirement building,
notifies the police, then tells the Mystery Club. They assume several
suspects: the manager of the Plaza, Dora's son Donald, or a Plaza
employee. Dora's husband, Ed Sutherland, is in Hawaii on board the
yacht Miss Chief with an all girl crew. Carrying on their own
investigation, the Mystery Club finally suspects Sutherland, though he
seems to have a perfect alibi. If they can prove it to their satisfaction,
will a court ever convict him-- if he can be found somewhere in the
Pacific?

THE MYSTERY CLUB AND THE DEAD DOCTOR

Second in the Mystery Club series. The Mystery Club consists of five
elderly women who live at the Rose Plaza and discuss mysteries written
by women. The Mystery Club ladies have no idea of the consequences
when Viola Cartwright, their blind member, asks them to go over her
Medicare bills. That leads to suspicion about the identity of her
personal assistant, Dorothy Anderson, who turns out to be using a
stolen identity. Viola's doctor runs a phony clinic owned by a member
of the Russian Mafia. Soon the investigation of Medicare bills leads to
murder and tragedy, stopped only by the courage of Mary Higgins.

THE MYSTERY CLUB AND THE HIDDEN WITNESS

Third in the Mystery Club series. The ladies of the Mystery Club
discover one of the residents is a crook under WITSEC, the witness

protection program. He apparently keeps dipping into the employee gift fund. The Mystery Club bands together to track down the missing money, but what they discover is danger.

THE MYSTERY CLUB AND THE SERIAL WIDOW

Fourth in the Mystery Club series. Caroline Kostinsky, new resident at the Rose Plaza, is a widow four times over and she's looking for a fifth husband in retired General Hardcastle, but when drunk she says she killed all of her husbands. Except for her confession, there's no evidence. Now what?

DELIVER ME FROM EVIL

Responding to a posted invitation for new members for the Mystery Club, Judge Ira Kahane and Ursula Besette show up. Ursula, at a turning point in her life as a new Rose Plaza resident, is interested in Wicca and Kabala. Roberta Nelson believes one should not suffer a witch to live. Judge Kahane tries to lead Ursula on the right path, but there is conflict and tragedy coming.

WHITE SLAVE

Sequel to *The Mystery Club Solves a Murder*. The appearance of Ed Sutherland's gold bracelet in a Portland pawn shop revives retired detective Casey's interest in the cold case. He doesn't know that Sutherland has been picked up and is a slave on a Korean fishing boat. Sutherland, penniless, .without clothes or identification, is stranded in New Zealand. Can he find his way back to Portland and be somehow redeemed or face a death sentence for first degree murder?

The Irwin Glass Series

BETRAYAL

Prequel to *Retribution.* Irwin Glass, BA in Russian, MA in International Relations, has a promising career in the Foreign Service in Moscow until he is snared in a classic "honey pot" seduction. He's young and naïve, honest, always wants to do the right thing, but at every turn he is betrayed. The incident in Moscow destroys his career. He is accused of being a paid Soviet agent and is pursued by the consequences of his encounter with the KGB twenty years later. Some enemies never let go

RETRIBUTION

Sequel to *Betrayal.* Newly married to Ivy Hartshorn, Irwin Glass gets a dunning letter from the IRS for taxes on interest at the Washington, DC account he didn't think he had. It's a joint account with his missing birth daughter and the balance is huge. Assuming it's money Katya's KGB father of record, Vladimir Putinsky (now Putin) deposited for her living expenses, Irwin moves it to force her to contact him. But Ivy warns him that he is laundering money and the people it belongs to will come after him. Irwin's complicated life is catching up with him, but this time he will find retribution.

BURNT OUT

Irwin Glass is approached by FBI Agent Wilkins who asks for Irwin's lists of foreign students. Not satisfied he wants more and is looking for potential terrorists among the Moslem students. Gradually Irwin is sucked into the role of FBI informant on the Michigan Institute of Technology's Muslim Students' Association and the results are tragic.

THE IRWIN GLASS TRILOGY

All three Irwin Glass books in one package deal. The Irwin Glass Trilogy combines all three of the Irwin Glass Mysteries: "Betrayal," "Retribution," and "Burnt Out," following the chaotic career of Irwin Glass who began, in "Betrayal," as a state department clerk in Moscow only to be caught in a classic honey pot seduction. Betrayed at every turn, he was sent back to the United States in disgrace to try to start a new life. No such luck. His teaching career is upturned by the revelation that the Moscow seduction had a consequence in the form of a beautiful student Katya who claims to be his daughter. In "Retribution," Irwin's KGB nemesis is in the United States seeking political asylum, but in fact is fleeing the Russian Mafia with Irwin as quarry. After "Retribution," Irwin thinks he is home free of all that intrigue, but the local FBI agent has a hold on him and wants information about potential terrorists among Irwin's students at Michigan Institute of Technology. There are risks to being a reluctant FBI informant, and Irwin's reports may be misconstrued with tragic results. What Irwin and his wife really want is a normal life, but his mysterious Russian birth daughter Katya remains an enigma. Is she or isn't she?

Other Mysteries

MURDER BY MAIL

German exchange student Klaus Hitz is more interested in making money than in asking questions about his work assignment. He doesn't know that the industrialist father of his punk girl friend is using him in a terrorist conspiracy to kill everyone in the United States with a mass mailing of a scratch and sniff virus. The plot begins to unravel when a Polish nurse brings blood samples from Libya and alerts a CIA agent. While the CIA and FBI track down the terrorists, Klaus Hitz gradually figures it out. How can he avoid being murdered or imprisoned for being naive?

MURDER IN THE KEWEENAW

CIA agent recovering from Post traumatic Stress after failed missions in Finland and a divorce is fishing in Lake Superior when he snags a corpse. He thinks he has seen the girl before and his attempt to identify her leads him to a ring of deadly pornographers. It almost costs him his own life.

CONSPIRACY!

Technical writer Tom Godot can't believe his luck when CONSPIRACY!, the book he has co-written with the elusive Harold Stevenson, is a hit. The book details a plot to hijack communication satellites. As Tom crosses the country on his book tour, he is disturbed by people interested in early drafts and dogged by an NSA agent. Communicating by fax with his editor and by encrypted e-mail with the mysterious Stevenson, Tom reaches out in his loneliness to his California girl friend Sylvia Hanson who turns out to be a pivotal figure. There is another conspiracy, and Tom is part of it

THE GOLD CHROMOSOME

When Adam Rottman's childless Aunt Sadie Gold died, the eight cousins learned her estate was in an irrevocable trust, the proceeds going to Adam's sister Sarah while she lives. After Sarah's death, the money would go to the last surviving cousin. It's a fatal tontine Adam's lawyer brother Harold set up. Would the cousins kill each other for one million dollars? Sarah's car is found in the river, but not Sarah. That begins a series of mysterious deaths. Coincidence? Or Murder? Who will be next? Adam and his psychologist wife Deborah must stop the chain before he, too, is eliminated.

BEN ZAKKAI'S COFFIN

Born of a Jewish father and a Catholic mother, Herman Bachrach insists he has no religion, but he is drawn by circumstance into a holocaust vendetta over gold stolen by a Swiss bank from Jewish depositors. Seduced by a woman who calls herself Diana, no last name, Herman is suspected by detective Sheehan to be her murderer. Someone else wants him dead. His Jewish boss provides him with a lawyer, but sends him to Switzerland to finish the job "Diana" started. It's an assignment he can't refuse. The result is an epiphany of identity that changes Herman's life forever.

THE LOLLIPOP MURDER

A warning for wannabe novelists! What happens when a stable of neurotic novelists who live in their pseudonyms and are bound by iron clad contracts are invited aboard their miserly Florida publisher's yacht for the Miami Book Fair only to find that they have no hope of ever earning a dime of royalties for their books? All this as Hurricane Gerta threatens to sink the yacht at the dock. It's grounds for murder

NOVELS

SAM IN LOVE

A coming of age romance for mature young adults. U.S. Army life in Europe in the 1950's was an equivalent of the Grand Tour of the eighteenth century when young men traveled and sowed wild oats. Marty, roommate of Sam Logan, a PFC draftee serving in the US Army in Munich, Germany, says all Sam needs is to get laid. Sam is not a virgin, but has a Midwestern ethic and believes in love. He doesn't know quite what that is. No Casanova, Sam, through a series of tentative encounters, thinks he's found the love of his life.

STOPRAPE.COM

Kerstin Mikkola, a young TV reporter at KDUP in Marquette, Michigan has hopes of a better network job. Her interview with a marine victim or rape might be just the ticket. Her interview about the web site StopRape.com goes viral on U-tube and Kerstin finds herself in the thick of consequences she did not anticipate.

THE ACCIDENTAL COURIER

A romance, road trip, and mystery all in one. Charles Kosko, retired orchard owner from Oregon, decides to take a bus trip in Europe and finds himself involved in a whistle-blower's scheme to discredit an American cell phone company that uses rare earths mined by slaves in the Congo. Unable to speak any foreign language, and without his US passport, he is picked up by a beautiful Israeli woman who says she is his driver. But is he really her prisoner? They are pursued by an African mining engineer, who hopes to intercept the delivery of stolen rare earths,

SCI-FI AND FANTASY

NEVER TRUST A TALKING HORSE

The narrator of this dystopian novel escapes preventive detention into a world he discovers has gone mad. Hungry, he is told he can eat for free at Lachumba's supper club, only to discover that he might be the main dish. He rescues Iris I. Iris from the ovens and in a series of episodes explores the insane world in search of a livelihood. He gradually realizes why he was incarcerated in the first place, but by then it is too late. His and Iris's roles have been reversed. Arrested, they are given a sadistic sentence which is their final challenge.

THE SEARCH FOR JESSE BRAM

Jesse Bram, the young hero of this metaphysical science fiction adventure, is unaware of his Jewish roots. An Eldre of mixed breed, he is marooned on the post apocalyptic shunned planet URth where technology and books have been destroyed. The URthlings variously view Jesse as a bringer of cargo for the half-breed prefect Hrod, as the reborn Savior by crypto-Christians, and as a link to the past by a remnant of Jews. The Galactic Federation suspects him of treason and he is pursued by an enigmatic Trinian policeman. If Jesse survives, will he be convicted? If acquitted, what next?

SHORT STORIES

THREADS OF THE COVENANT: THE JEWS OF RED JACKET

A collection of twenty-one short stories about Jewish life in small town America centering about two main characters, David Katz, the only Jewish boy in Red Jacket, and Richard Goldman, the only Jewish professor at Copper country Community College. Each story depicts another aspect of what it means to be a Jew in a small town as each character comes to realize his own identity.

MISPLACED PERSONS

Though set in different locales what these stories have in common is a central character who is out of his element, in the wrong place, coming to grips with cultural, generational, or physical displacement. In PROBLEM FOR THE TEACHER an expatriate fumbles for a living; in LIMBO an ex-G.I. is adrift in Copenhagen; in TRIUMPH OF THE WILL a nervous wreck seeks recuperation; in MISCALCULATION a would be tax evader succumbs to his own fears; in THE LIE a drunk gets himself into difficulties, and in THE GIRLS OF FREDERIKSHAVN an old man is trapped by girls looking for action.

YOOPER TALES AND OTHER FUNNY STUFF

Extracted from the massive volume of Sachs's published Essays and Columns: 1992-2011, this collection of stories related to Michigan's Upper Peninsula, known as the UP, home of Yoopers, reveals the truth about snow fleas, ice worms, the humungous fungus (world's largest living thing) and the rigors of winters in the remote north woods. You can also learn how to catch and cook the Mosquito Giganticus and why visitors won't come. Sachs has several awards for his humor.

AHOY! QUARTERDECK!

Originally published as IRMA QUARTERDECK REPORTS but re-released with new illustrations and, in the paperback edition, with sea shanties, this funny book is a series of boating anecdotes about Irma and her bumbling husband Ralph ("I can't believe I lost the anchor") Quarterdeck in their many boating adventures and mishaps. One reviewer says the book is as informative as Chapman's famous manual, but more fun. Readers will find plenty of laughs in this book and at the same time learn a great deal of boating fundamentals.

ANNA-LENA'S TROLL AND OHER STORIES

Each of the three Sachs daughters has a story in this children's book. "Anna-Lena's Troll" explores the nature of trolls, which represent the dark side of human behavior as Anna-Lena's nasty letter to Santa is rewarded by the gift of a nasty troll. "The Return of Baby Suzy" is the true story of Cynthia's worn out doll and its resurrection. "The Stars for Christmas" is the remarkable surprise Belinda got along with her new eye glasses. Other family stories are Christmas related.

NON-FICTION

THE MISADVENTURES OF CPL. SACHS

Adrift through college at Indiana University, author Sachs was drafted at the end of the Korean War. Physically unfit for combat, he was sent to Queer Company for basic training, then by a fluke was shipped out to Germany instead of Korea. Thus began his own version of the traditional Grand Tour.

FREELANCE NONFICTION ARTICLES

This third edition of a monograph on freelance writing first published by the Society for Technical Communication is newly updated. This little manual provides tips for interviewing, article structure, article preparation and submission, photography, and business practice.

CHILLY-CHILLY-BANG—HOW WE FREELANCED THROUGH EUROPE'S COLDEST WINTER IN A VW WITH A KID

Companion piece to *Freelance Nonfiction Articles*. The former is a how to book. This is a "how we did it" memoir. The author knew nothing about Volkswagens when they set off, but as they worked from VW dealer to dealer getting the old Combi fixed, he learned! It's as much a book for VW enthusiasts as it is for writers.

Both FREELANCE NONFICTION ARTICLES and *Chilly-Chilly-BANG! How we Freelanced Through Europe's Coldest Winter in a VW with a Kid* are combined in a double volume, *The Writing Life*.

THE 1957 SACHS ARCTIC EXPEDITION

After military service in Germany the author took the GI Bill to Sweden. With no income in the summer, and not even sure there was a road to the far north, he set off hitchhiking to North Cape, the northernmost point in Europe in search of the midnight sun. Illustrated.

FROM TENT TO CASTLE: MEMOIR OF A YEAR LONG HONEYMOON

Setting off from Stockholm, Sweden on rebuilt one speed bicycles, Harley and Ulla embarked on an open-ended honeymoon with no fixed destination and equipped with a tent, a thin double sleeping bag, a tiny gasoline stove, and $3000. After arriving in Britain, Ulla discovered she was pregnant. Tired of unrelenting rain, they advertised for a cheap place to spend the winter. They were offered the gatehouse to Borthwick Castle outside Edinburgh, Scotland for $25 a month by British author Theo Lang.

"IS"

As Bill Clinton said, "It all depends on what the meaning of "is" is."

A problem we all have is distinguishing between what is real and what is not. This is in fact an age-old question. This volume switches between classical instances of the problem to the author and his psychiatrist and his wife. What is real? That all depends on the meaning of "real."

QUEER COMPANY

Not a gay novel, this is a fictionalized memoir of an experimental basic training unit at the end of the Korean War. All the draftees were physically unfit for combat but the army didn't want to discharge them. Instead they got modified training in a company unfortunately designated Q. In the Army phonetic alphabet Q is Queen, but Q company was called queer. A copy is in the US Army historical archives.

The Lollipop Murder